Maigret and the Saturday Caller

Georges Simenon

Maigret and the
Saturday Caller

Translated by Tony White

A Harvest Book • Harcourt, Inc.

A Helen and Kurt Wolff Book

Orlando   Austin   New York   San Diego   Toronto   London

www.HarcourtBooks.com

This is a translation of *Maigret et le client du samedi.*

Maigret is a registered trademark of the Estate of Georges Simenon.

Library of Congress Cataloging-in-Publication Data
Simenon, Georges, 1903–1989.
[Maigret et le client due samedi. English]
Maigret and the Saturday Caller/Georges Simenon; translated
by Tony White. — 1st ed.
p. cm.
ISBN 0-15-602842-5
Translation of: Maigret et le client du samedi.
"A Helen and Kurt Wolff Book."
I. Title.
PQZ637.I53M257913   1991
843'.912—dc20   90-46032

Printed in the United States of America
First Harvest edition 1992
A C E G I J H F D B

1

Certain images, for no apparent reason, and without our having anything to do with it, stay with us, stuck obstinately in our memories, even though we are hardly aware of having recorded them and they are not important. In this way, no doubt, years later, Maigret would be able to reconstruct, minute by minute, move by move, that uneventful late afternoon at the Quai des Orfèvres.

First, there was the black marble clock with bronze hands. When he glanced at it, it said eighteen minutes before six o'clock, which meant that it was really just after six. In a dozen other offices in the Police Judiciaire, in the director's as well as in those of the inspectors, identical clocks stood flanked by candelabra, and, from time immemorial, they, too, had been slow.

Why did this thought strike him today more than any other? For a moment he wondered how many governments or ministries this F. Ledent, whose fine copperplate signature was on the pale dial, had supplied with a consignment of such clocks, and he imagined the bargaining, intrigue, and petty bribery that must have gone on before such an important transaction.

F. Ledent had been dead for half a century, maybe a whole century, judging by the style of his clocks.

The lamp with the green shade was on, because it was January. The lamps in the rest of the building were on, too.

Lucas was standing by him, slipping the documents Maigret had just passed to him one by one into a yellow folder.

"Shall I leave Janvier at the Crillon?"

"Not too late. Send someone to relieve him this evening."

There had been a series of jewel robberies, one right after another, as is always the case, from the deluxe hotels on the Champs-Elysées, and a discreet watch was being kept on each of them.

Maigret automatically pressed an electric bell. It wasn't long before old Joseph, the PJ clerk with the silver chain, opened the door.

"Anyone else for me?" the chief inspector asked.

"Only the madwoman."

She was not important. For months, she had been coming two or three times a week to the Quai des Orfèvres, slipping, without a word, into the waiting room and settling down to her knitting. She had never given her name. The first time, Joseph had asked her whom she wanted to see.

She had given him a wicked, almost saucy smile and replied:

"Inspector Maigret will send for me when he needs me."

Joseph had given her a form. She had filled it out in a neat hand that suggested a convent education. Her name was Clémentine Pholien and she lived on Rue Lamarck.

That time, the chief had had Janvier see her.

"Were you sent for?"

"Inspector Maigret knows about it."

"Did he send you a summons?"

She smiled. She was a slight, graceful woman, in spite of her age.

"There's no need for a summons."

"Have you something to tell him?"

"Perhaps."

"He's very busy just now."

"Never mind. I'll wait."

She had waited until seven in the evening and then gone away. They had seen her again a few days later, with the same mauve hat, the same knitting, and she had taken her seat, like a regular, in the glassed-in waiting room.

They had made inquiries, just in case. She had been running a notions shop in Montmartre for some time, and she derived a comfortable income from it. Her nephews and nieces had tried several times to have her put in an institution, but each time, she had been discharged from the psychiatric hospital because she was not dangerous.

Where had she got hold of Maigret's name? She didn't know him by sight, because he had passed the "glass cage" several times while she was there, and she hadn't recognized him.

"Well, Lucas, we'll shut up shop!"

They were closing down early, especially for a Saturday. The chief filled his pipe and got his coat, hat, and scarf from his closet.

As he passed the glass cage, he carefully looked away. Down in the yard, he ran into somewhat yellowish fog, which had descended on Paris during the afternoon.

He was in no hurry. With his coat collar turned up and his hands in his pockets, he circled the Palais de Justice, passed under the big clock, and crossed the Pont-au-Change. Halfway across the bridge, he had the feeling that someone was following him and he turned around sharply. There were lots of people going in both directions. Because of the cold, nearly all of them were walking quickly. But he was almost sure that a man in dark clothing, about ten yards away, suddenly turned around.

He didn't pay much attention to it. It was, after all, only an impression.

A few minutes later, he was waiting for his bus in Place du Châtelet, and he found room on the rear platform, where he could continue smoking his pipe. Did it really have an unusual taste? He could have sworn it had. Perhaps it was because of the fog, or of some quality in the air. A pleasant taste.

He wasn't thinking of anything in particular. He was day-dreaming and vaguely studying his neighbors' nodding heads.

Then he took to the sidewalk again, along almost-deserted Boulevard Richard-Lenoir, toward the lights of his apartment, which he could pick out from a distance. He started up the familiar stairs, past the bright strips of light under the doors, and heard muffled voices and the sound of radios.

His door opened, as usual, before he had touched the knob. Madame Maigret, framed against the light, was mysteriously holding a finger to her lips.

He looked at her questioningly, trying to see behind her.

"There's someone . . ." she whispered.

"Who?"

"I don't know. He's peculiar."

"What did he tell you?"

"That he simply had to speak to you."

"What's he like?"

"I can't explain, but his breath smells of drink."

There was quiche lorraine for supper, he could tell by the odor coming from the kitchen.

"Where is he?"

"I showed him into the living room."

She helped him off with his coat, hat, and scarf. The apartment seemed less brightly lit than usual, but no doubt that was a false impression. With a shrug, he pushed open the door of the living room, where, for just over a month, a television set had held pride of place.

The man had remained standing, in his coat, holding his hat. He seemed nervous and hardly dared to look at the chief inspector.

"You must forgive me for following you home," he stammered.

Maigret immediately noticed his harelip. He did not mind finding himself face to face with the man at last.

"You've been to see me at the Quai des Orfèvres, haven't you?"

"Several times, yes."

"Your name's . . . Just a minute. Planchon."

"Léonard Planchon, that's right."

He repeated, even more humbly:

"You must forgive me."

His glance traveled around the small living room and stopped at the door, which was half-open, as if he wanted to run away again. How many times had he already gone away like that without meeting the chief inspector?

At least five. It was always a Saturday afternoon. They had nicknamed him "the Saturday caller."

He was like the madwoman, but with a difference. The Police Judiciaire, like newspaper offices, attracts all sorts of somewhat weird people. The employees come to know their faces well.

"I wrote to you first . . . " he murmured.

"Sit down."

Through a glass door, the table, set for a meal, was visible. The man glanced in its direction.

"Isn't it your suppertime?"

5

"Sit down," Maigret repeated with a sigh.

He had got home early for once, yet his dinner would still be late. So much for the quiche! And the television news! For some weeks, he and his wife had watched television while they ate, and they had changed their places at the table in order to see it.

"You say you've written to me?"

"At least ten letters."

"Signed with your name?"

"The first weren't signed. I tore them up. I tore up the others, too. That's when I decided to go and see you."

Maigret, too, recognized the smell of alcohol, but his visitor was not drunk. On edge, yes. His fingers were so tightly clenched that they were white at the joints. Only gradually did he dare look at the chief inspector, with an almost pleading expression.

What age was he? It was hard to say. He was neither young nor old; in fact, he looked as if he had never been young. Thirty-five?

It wasn't easy, either, to guess which social class he belonged to. His clothes were poorly cut, but of good quality, and his hands, though very clean, were those of a manual worker.

"Why did you tear up those letters?"

"I was afraid you might think I was crazy."

Then, looking up, he added, as if he needed to convince the chief inspector:

"I'm not crazy, Monsieur Maigret. I beg you to believe that I'm not."

This was usually a bad sign, yet Maigret was already half-convinced. He could hear his wife moving around in the kitchen. She must have taken the quiche out of the oven. It would be spoiled now, anyway.

"So you wrote me several letters. Then you turned up at the Quai des Orfèvres. A Saturday, I think?"

"It's the only day I'm free."

"What do you do for a living, Monsieur Planchon?"

"I own a painting and decorating firm. Oh, very small. When it's doing well, I sometimes employ five or six men. Do you understand?"

Because of his harelip, it was difficult to tell if he was smiling shyly or making a face. His eyes were very pale blue and his fair hair slightly reddish.

"This first visit was about two months ago. You wrote on the form that you wanted to see me personally. Why?"

"Because you're the only person I can trust. I've read in the papers . . ."

"Yes. Well, that Saturday, instead of waiting, you went off after about ten minutes."

"I was afraid."

"Of what?"

"I thought you wouldn't take me seriously. Or that you'd stop me from doing what I'd planned."

"You came back the following Saturday."

"Yes."

Maigret had been in conference that day with his boss and two other inspectors. When he had come out, an hour later, the waiting room was empty.

"You were still afraid?"

"I didn't know. . . ."

"What didn't you know?"

"If I still wanted to go through with it."

He wiped his forehead.

"It's all so complicated. You see, there are times when I don't know where I am."

On another Saturday, Maigret had sent Lucas to see him.

The man had refused to disclose the purpose of his visit, insisting that it was personal. Then he had literally fled.

"Who gave you my address?"

"I followed you. Last Saturday I nearly stopped you in the street. Then I decided that it wasn't a suitable place for the sort of conversation I wanted with you. Or in your office. Perhaps you understand now?"

"How did you know I was coming home tonight?"

Maigret suddenly remembered his feeling on the Pont-au-Change.

"You were hiding on the quai, weren't you?"

Planchon nodded.

"Did you follow me to the bus?"

"That's right. Then I took a taxi and arrived here a few minutes ahead of you."

"Are you in trouble, Monsieur Planchon?"

"Worse than trouble."

"How many drinks did you have before you came here?"

"Two. Maybe three. Before, I never used to drink, hardly even a glass of wine at meals."

"And now?"

"It depends what day it is. Or, what evening. Because I don't drink in the daytime. Except, just now, I drank three brandies to give me courage. . . . Are you angry with me?"

Maigret was puffing his pipe slowly, his eyes fixed on his visitor, trying to make up his mind about him. He had not yet succeeded. He suspected that there was a pathetic side to Planchon, and it baffled him. The man gave an impression of suppressed, overwhelming misery, and, at the same time, of extraordinary patience.

He would have staked his last penny that Planchon had few contacts with his fellow-men, and that everything went on inside him. For two months, he had been tortured by the need to speak. He had tried, Saturday after Saturday, to see the chief inspector, and, each time, he had at last left.

"Suppose you tell me your story."

Another glance at the dining room, where the two places were set facing the televison set.

"I feel bad keeping you from eating. It will take some time. Your wife will be cross with me, I know! If you don't mind, I'll wait here until you've eaten. Or I'll come back later. That's it! I'll come back later."

He started to get up, and the chief inspector had to force him to keep his seat.

"No, Monsieur Planchon! You've made it this time, haven't you? Tell me what's on your mind. Tell me straight out what you wrote in all those letters you tore up."

Then, staring at the red-patterned carpet, the man stammered:

"I want to kill my wife."

Suddenly, he looked up at the chief inspector, who had, with some difficulty, managed not to give a start.

"You intend to kill your wife?"

"I must. There's no other way out. I don't know how to explain. Every evening I tell myself that it'll happen, that it's impossible for it not to happen one day or other. So I thought that if I told you about it . . ."

He pulled a handkerchief out of his pocket and wiped the lenses of his glasses, searching for words. Maigret noticed that one of his coat buttons was hanging on by a thread.

In spite of his nervousness, Planchon caught Maigret's quick glance, and gave a smile, or made a face.

"Yes. That's another thing." he muttered. "She doesn't even pretend to . . ."

"Pretend to what?"

"Look after me. Be my wife."

Was he sorry he had come? He was fidgeting on his chair and occasionally glancing at the door, as if he might suddenly dash through it.

"I wonder if I was wrong. Yet you're the only man in the world I trust. I feel I've known you for ages. I'm almost sure you'll understand."

"Are you jealous, Monsieur Planchon?"

Their eyes met directly. Maigret sensed complete honesty in the face of the man opposite him.

"I don't think I am any longer. I was. No! It's all over, now."

"Yet you still want to kill her?"

"Because there's no other solution. So I thought that if I warned you, by letter or in person . . . First, it would be more honest. Then, perhaps, if I did that, I might change my mind. Do you understand? No! You can't understand if you don't know Renée. Forgive me if I seem muddled. Renée's my wife. My daughter's Isabelle. She's seven. She's all I have left in the world. You don't have any children, do you?"

He looked around once again, to make sure there were no toys lying around, or any of those thousand and one things that reveal a child's presence in a house.

"They want to take her away from me, too. They're doing everything they can. They make no secret of it. I wish you could see how they treat me. Do you think I'm off my head?"

"No."

"Mind you, it would be better. I'd be put away immediately. Just as if I'd killed my wife. Or if I killed him. The best thing would be to kill the pair of them. But then, if I was in prison, who'd look after Isabelle? Do you see the problem?

"I've thought up complicated plans. I've hit on at least ten, and carefully worked them out down to the last detail. It's a question of not being found out. People would think they'd gone away together. I read in a paper that thousands of women in Paris disappear every year, and that the police don't bother to look for them. All the more unlikely, if he disappeared at the same time as her.

"Look! I even decided, at one time, where I'd hide the bodies. I was working on a site way up above Montmartre. Where they make precast concrete. I'd drive them away at night in my van, and no one would ever find them."

He was getting worked up, but was now talking fairly freely, though he kept a close watch on the chief inspector's reactions.

"Has anyone ever come and told you he intended to kill his wife, or anyone else, before?"

This was so unexpected that Maigret had to rack his brain.

"Not like this," he finally admitted.

"Do you think I'm lying or making up a story to seem interesting?"

"No."

"Do you believe I really want to kill my wife?"

"You obviously intend to."

"And that I'll do it?"

"No."

"Why not?"

"Because you came to see me."

Planchon got up, too on edge, too tense to remain seated. He raised his arms to the ceiling.

"That's what I think, too!" he almost sobbed. "That's why I went away, each time, before seeing you. That's why I needed to talk to you, too. I'm not a criminal. I'm a law-abiding man. And yet . . ."

At this point, Maigret went and got the decanter of calvados from the sideboard and poured a glass for his visitor.

"Aren't you having any?" the man murmured, ashamed.

Then he glanced toward the dining room.

"Of course! You haven't had supper yet. And I'm talking and not making sense. I want to explain everything all at once and I don't know where to begin."

"Would you rather I asked you questions?"

"It might be easier."

"Sit down quietly."

"I'll try."

"How long have you been married?"

"Eight years."

"Did you live alone?"

"Yes. I've always been alone. Ever since my mother died when I was fifteen. We lived on Rue de Picpus, not far from here. She used to go out to clean."

"And your father?"

"I never knew him."

He had blushed.

"Did you become an apprentice?"

"Yes. I became a painter-decorator. I was twenty-six when my boss, who lived on Rue Tholozé, found out he had a heart disease and decided to retire to the country."

"Did you take over the business?"

"I had some savings. But even so, it took me six years to pay off the cost."

"Where did you meet your wife?"

"Do you know Rue Tholozé? It leads into Rue Lepic, right in front of the Moulin de la Galette. It's a dead end, at a few steps. I live by the steps, in a small house in a yard, which is handy for ladders and supplies."

He was calming down. His speech was now more measured, flatter.

"About halfway along the street, on the left-hand side, there's a little dance hall, the Bal des Copains, where I sometimes used to spend an hour or two on Saturday evening."

"Did you dance?"

"No. I used to sit in a corner and order a lemonade, because I didn't drink then. I used to listen to the music and watch the couples."

"Did you have any girlfriends?"

He answered bashfully:

"No."

"Why not?"

He pointed to his lip.

"I'm not good-looking. Women have always scared me. I feel my lip must put them off."

"Then you met one named Renée?"

"Yes. There was a big crowd that evening. We were put at the same table. I didn't dare speak to her. But she was as scared as I was. You could tell she wasn't used to . . ."

"Dances?"

"Dances, everything . . . Paris. Finally, she spoke to me, and I found out that she'd only been in town a month. I asked her where she came from. She said Saint-Sauveur, near Fontenay-le-Comte in the Vendée, which happens to be my mother's town. When I was a child, I went there several times with her to see my aunts and uncles. That's what made things easy. We kept mentioning names we both knew."

"What was Renée doing in Paris?"

"She was general helper at a dairy on Rue Lepic."

"Was she younger than you?"

"I'm thirty-six and she's twenty-seven. That makes nearly ten years' difference. She was barely eighteen at the time."

"Did you get married right away?"

"It took about ten months. Then we had a baby, a little girl, Isabelle. All the time my wife was pregnant, I was very frightened."

"Of what?"

Once again he pointed to his harelip.

"They had told me it was hereditary. Thank heaven, my

daughter's normal! She's like her mother, except that she's got my fair hair and pale eyes."

"Is your wife dark?"

"Like lots of people from the Vendée, because, apparently, of the Portuguese, who used to fish there."

"So now you want to kill her?"

"I don't see any alternative. We were happy, the three of us. Renée wasn't much of a housewife, maybe. I don't want to run her down. She spent her childhood on a farm, where no one bothered about things being neat and clean. Down there in the marshes, they call the houses 'cabins,' and sometimes, in the winter, the water flows right into the rooms."

"I know."

"Have you been there?"

"Yes."

"I often used to do the housework at the end of the day. At that time, she was crazy about the cinema. In the afternoon, she'd leave Isabelle with the concierge so she could go see a film."

He spoke without bitterness.

"I didn't grumble. I couldn't forget that she was the first woman to treat me like a normal man. You understand that, too, don't you?"

He no longer dared to turn toward the dining room.

"Here! I *am* keeping you from your supper. What will your wife think?"

"Go on. How many years were you happy?"

"Just a minute. I've never counted. I don't even quite know when it all began. I had a nice little business. I spent what I earned putting the house in shape, repainting it, modernizing it, fixing up an attractive kitchen. You should come and . . . But you won't. Or if you do, it would mean that . . ."

Once again he gripped his fingers, which were covered with red hairs.

"You probably don't know the business. At times, you have plenty of work, and at others, hardly any. It's difficult to keep the same workers. Except for old Jules, the one we call 'Pépère,' who worked for my old boss, I changed them almost every year."

"Until the day . . ."

"Until the day Roger Prou joined me. He's a good-looking fellow, strong and shrewd, who knows what he's doing. At first, I was delighted to have a man like him, because I could trust him completely on a job."

"Did he make advances to your wife?"

"I don't honestly think so. He could have had as many women as he wanted, even customers sometimes. I can't say, because, at the beginning, I didn't notice anything. But I'm almost sure it was Renée who began it. It's not just that I'm disfigured, but I'm not the sort of man a woman enjoys herself with."

"What do you mean?"

"Nothing, really. I'm not very cheerful. I don't care for going out. What I like in the evenings is to stay at home, and on Sundays to go for a walk with my wife and daughter. . . . For months, I didn't suspect anything. When we were out on a job, Prou used to be the one to go back to Rue Tholozé to get supplies. Once, when I returned unexpectedly—it was two years ago—I found my daughter alone in the kitchen. I can still see her. She was sitting on the floor. I asked her: 'Where's Maman?' "

"She answered, pointing to the bedroom: 'There!'

"She was only five at the time. They hadn't heard me come in, and I caught them half-naked. Prou seemed embarrassed. But my wife looked me straight in the eye.

15

" 'Well, now you know!' she said."

"What did you do?"

"I left. I didn't know where I was going or what I was doing. I found myself leaning on a bar, and I got drunk for the first time in my life. I was thinking mostly about my daughter. I promised myself I'd take her away. I kept saying to myself: 'She's yours! They have no right to keep her.'

"Then, after wandering half the night, I went home. I'd been sick. My wife gave me a black look and when I was sick on the carpet, she muttered: 'You disgust me.'

"There you are! That's how it all began. The day before, I was a happy man. All of a sudden . . ."

"Where's Roger Prou?"

"On Rue Tholozé," Planchon stammered, looking down.

"For the last two years?"

"Just about, yes."

"Does he live with your wife?"

"The three of us live . . ."

He tried to wipe his glasses again and blinked.

"Does it seem incredible to you?"

"No."

"Do you understand why I couldn't leave her?"

"Leave your wife?"

"At first, I stayed on for her. Now, I don't know. I think it's only for my daughter. But maybe I'm wrong. You see, I couldn't bear the thought of life without Renée. Or the idea of being alone again. And I had no right to throw her out. I was the one who begged her to marry me. I was responsible for it, wasn't I?"

He sniffed and glanced sideways at the decanter. Maigret helped him to a second glass, which he downed at a gulp.

"You'll be thinking I'm a drunkard. Mind you, I've nearly become one. They don't like seeing me around the house in the evenings. They practically shove me out. You have no idea how mean they are to me."

"Prou settled in at your place from the very day you caught them?"

"No. Not right away. The next morning, I was surprised to see him go on with his job as if nothing had happened. I didn't dare ask him what he had in mind. I was afraid of losing her, as I told you. I didn't know where I stood. I walked carefully. I'm sure they went on seeing each other, and soon, they stopped being careful with me. I was the one who hesitated about coming back, who made a noise to warn them.

"One evening, he stayed to dinner. It was his birthday, and Renée had cooked a good meal. There was a bottle of champagne on the table. During dessert, my wife asked me: 'Don't you want to go out for a while? Don't you realize you're in the way?'

"So I went out. I drank. I asked myself questions. I tried to answer them. I told myself stories. I wasn't thinking of killing them then, I assure you. Tell me you believe me. Tell me you don't think I'm crazy. Tell me I'm not the hateful creature my wife makes out I am!"

Madame Maigret passed back and forth on the other side of the glass door. Planchon whined:

"I'm keeping you from your supper. Your wife will be cross. Why don't you go and eat?"

It was too late for the news, anyway.

2

Two or three times, Maigret had been tempted to pinch himself, to make sure that the man sitting in front of him was real, that the scene was actually taking place, and that they were both living people.

At first sight, he was an ordinary man, one of the modest striving millions you rub shoulders with every day in the Métro, in buses, on the sidewalk, heading for some unknown job and fate, soberly and with dignity. Paradoxically, his harelip made him more impersonal, as if the blemish gave all those afflicted with it identical faces.

For a second or two, the chief inspector wondered if Planchon had not, as some kind of diabolical plan, deliberately chosen to come and wait for him on Boulevard Richard-Lenoir, instead of seeing him in his prosaic office at the Quai des Orfèvres. Was it not, perhaps, intuition that had made him leave the glassed-in waiting room, and its walls covered with the photographs of policemen killed in the line of duty?

At the Police Judiciaire, where he had heard thousands of

confessions, and where he had tricked so many people into heartbreaking disclosures, Maigret would have seen his visitor in a cold light.

But here, he was at home, in a familiar atmosphere, with Madame Maigret nearby, the smell of supper waiting, the furniture, the ornaments, the tiniest reflections of light in the same places they had been for years and years. He would hardly be through the door before it all enveloped him, like an old jacket you put on when you get home, and he was so used to this setting that, even after a month, he still resented the television set installed opposite the glass door of the dining room.

Would he conduct as clear and detached an interrogation in this atmosphere as in his office, one of those interrogations that sometimes lasted hours, sometimes the whole night, and which used to leave him as exhausted as the victim?

For the first time in his entire career, a man had sought him out here, after putting it off for weeks, after following him in the street, after writing to him, so he said, after tearing up his letters, and after waiting for him for hours in the glass cage. A man, unremarkable in dress and appearance, had entered his home, humbly yet obstinately, to say in so many words:

"I intend to kill two people: my wife and her lover. To this end, I have planned everything, worked it out to the last detail, to avoid being caught. . . ."

And now, instead of reacting skeptically, Maigret was listening to him with intense concentration, not missing one of his changes of expression. He had almost stopped regretting the variety show he had planned to watch on television that evening, sitting beside his wife, because they were still new to it, and everything that happened on that little screen fascinated them.

What was more, when the man indicated Madame Maigret moving about in the dining room, he had almost said:

"Come and have a bite with us."

He was hungry, but he thought it might take some time. He needed to know more, to ask questions, and to make sure he was not mistaken.

Two or three times, his visitor, racked with doubt, had asked him:

"You don't think I'm crazy, do you?"

He had thought about this possibility, too. There are varying degrees of madness, he knew by experience, and the tired notions seller who came smiling into the waiting room, to knit away until he needed her, was just one example.

This man had been drinking before he'd come. He admitted that he drank every evening, and Maigret had given him calvados because he needed it.

Alcoholics plunge readily into a world of their own, one similar to the real world but with certain aberrations not always easy to detect. And they are sincere.

These ideas had flashed through his head as he was listening, but none of them satisfied him. He was trying to understand how to force his way into Planchon's bewildering little world.

"That was how I started to feel left out," said the man, still looking at him with his pale eyes. "I don't know how to explain. . . . I loved her. I think I still do. Yes, I'm almost sure I still love her, and I'll go on loving her, even if I have to kill her.

"Aside from my mother, she's the only person who ever took an interest in me, and didn't worry about my infirmity.

"Besides, she's my wife. Whatever she does, she's my wife, isn't she? She gave me Isabelle. She carried her in her womb. You have no idea what I went through while she was pregnant. I used to kneel down in front of her, and thank her for . . .

I don't know how to say it. Part of my life was in her. Do you understand? And Isabelle is part of both of us.

"Before, I was alone. No one looked after me. No one waited for me in the evening. I worked without a reason.

"Then, all of a sudden, she'd taken a lover. And I couldn't really blame her. She's young. She's attractive.

"Also, Roger Prou's more manly than I am. He's like an animal, bursting with good health and strength."

Madame Maigret had given up and returned to the kitchen. Maigret slowly filled another pipe.

"I kept arguing with myself. I kept on telling myself that it wouldn't last, that she'd come back to me, and that she'd realize that we were tied to each other, whatever she did. Am I boring you?"

"No. Go on."

"I don't quite know what I'm saying. I think it was clearer in my letters, and not half so long.

"If I'd still been going to church, as I did when my mother was alive, I'd definitely have gone to confession. I don't remember how I came to think of you. At first, I didn't believe I'd have the courage to come and see you.

"Now that I'm here, I want to get it all off my chest. I promise you that I'm not talking so much because I've been drinking. I worked out everything I was going to say. . . .

"Where was I?"

He was blinking and fiddling with a small brass ashtray, which he'd idly picked up from a small table.

"On the evening of Prou's birthday, they threw you out. . . ."

"Well, not exactly, because they knew I'd come back. They sent me out so they could spend the evening alone together."

"Were you still hoping it would be only a phase?"

"Do you think I'm so naïve?"

"What happened after that?"

He gave a sigh and shook his head, like a man who has lost track of his thoughts.

"So much! A few days after his birthday, when I sat home, about two or three in the morning, I found a cot set up in the dining room. At first, I didn't realize it was for me. I half opened the door of the bedroom. They were both in our one bed, asleep, or pretending to be.

"What could I do? Roger Prou's stronger than I am. Besides, I wasn't very steady on my legs. I was convinced he'd probably strike me.

"And also, I didn't want Isabelle to wake up. She doesn't understand yet. In her eyes, I'm still her father.

"I slept on the cot. When they got up, in the morning, I was already at work.

"My workmen gave me some odd leers. But old Jules, the one with the white hair we call 'Pépère,' reacted differently. He was in the business before me—I think I told you. He calls me by my Christian name. He came and found me in the workshop and muttered: 'Look, Léonard, it's about time you threw that bitch out. If you don't act now, it'll end in disaster.'

"He knew that I didn't have the courage. He looked me in the eyes, one hand on my shoulder, and concluded, with a sigh: 'I didn't realize you were as sick as all that. . . .'

"I wasn't sick. It was just that I still loved her, needed her, her company, even if she was sleeping with someone else.

"I must ask you to answer me frankly, Monsieur Maigret."

He didn't say, "Chief Inspector," as he would have at the Quai des Orfèvres, but "Monsieur Maigret," as if he wanted to underline the fact that it was the man he had come to see.

"Have you ever run across a case like mine?"

"Are you asking me if other men stay with their wives even though they know they have lovers?"

"Something of the sort."

22

"Lots do."

"Only I suppose their place in the home is kept, or at least there's some pretense made that they matter. Not in mine. For almost two years now they've been slowly pushing me out. They hardly even set my place at the table. It's not Prou who's the stranger; it's me. During meals, they chat together, laugh, and talk to my daughter as if I were some sort of ghost.

"On Sundays, they take the van and drive out to the country. At first, I stayed with Isabelle and always used to find some way of amusing her.

"If it weren't for Isabelle, I might have gone away. I don't know.

"But my daughter often goes with them now, because it's more fun to go for a car-ride.

"I've asked myself every question you can think of, not only in the evenings, when I've had a few drinks, but in the mornings, and all day while I'm working. I still work hard.

"Emotional questions and practical questions. Three months ago I even went and saw a lawyer. I didn't tell him as much as I've told you, because I felt he wasn't really listening to me, and that he was getting impatient.

" 'So what do you really want?' he asked me.

" 'I don't know.'

" 'A divorce?'

" 'I don't know. The thing I want most is to keep my daughter.'

" 'Have you any proof of your wife's misconduct?'

" 'I've told you that, every night, I sleep on a cot, while the two of them are in my room.'

" 'It would have to be checked by the police. Under what code were you married?'

"He explained to me that, since we hadn't signed a marriage contract, Renée and I were married under the joint-estate system, which means that my business, my house, my furniture, everything I own, including the clothes I have on, are just as much hers as mine.

" 'What about my daughter?' I went on. 'Would they give me my daughter?'

" 'That depends. If misconduct is proved and if the judge . . .' "

He gritted his teeth.

"He told me something else," he went on after a moment. "Before I went to see him, just as I did before I came here, I had a drink or two to buck me up. He noticed it right away. I knew this by the way he treated me.

" 'The judge will decide which of you is better able to provide your daughter with a normal life.'

"My wife said the same thing, in other words. 'What's stopping you from going away?' she said several times. 'Haven't you any self-respect? Don't you realize you're not wanted here?'

"Each time, I answered, stubbornly: 'I'll never abandon my daughter.'

" 'She's mine, too, isn't she? Do you think I'd let her go off with a drunkard like you?'

"I'm not a drunkard, Monsieur Maigret. I beg you to believe me, in spite of appearances. I never drank before all this, not even a drop. But what could I do in the evenings, all alone in the streets?

"I started going into bistros and leaning on the bar, just to feel people around me, and hear people talking, human voices.

"I'd have one drink, then another. That always started me thinking, and that makes me want to drink another and another.

"I tried to stop. I felt so ill that I wanted to go and throw myself in the Seine. I thought about it a lot. It was the easiest way out. It was Isabelle who stopped me. I didn't and still don't want to leave her to them. It's the thought that one day she might call him Papa."

He was now crying quite unashamedly. He pulled his handkerchief out of his pocket. Maigret continued watching him stolidly.

There was obviously some aberration. Whether drunk or not, the man was becoming hysterical, purposely giving way to despair.

From a strict police angle, there was nothing to do. The man had done nothing wrong. He intended to kill his wife and her lover—at least so he said. But he had not informed them of his intention, so there was not even a threat of death.

From the legal point of view, all the chief inspector could have said to him was:

"Come back afterward."

When at last he was guilty! He could have added, with little fear of correction:

"If you tell your story to the jury as you've just told it to me, and if you have a good lawyer, you'll probably be acquitted."

Was this the solution Planchon had, in some sense, come to wheedle out of him? For a few moments, Maigret suspected him. He did not like men who gave way to tears. He was suspicious of those who confessed easily, and this emotional display, exaggerated by drink, certainly irritated him.

He had already missed his dinner and the news and variety show. Yet Planchon showed no sign of going. He seemed to be enjoying the warm atmosphere, too. Was he going to be like one of those stray dogs you pat as you pass by and then cannot get rid of?

"I'm sorry," Planchon finally stammered, wiping his eyes. "You must think me absurd. It's the first time in my life I've confided in anyone."

Maigret was tempted to reply:

"Why in me?"

But he knew it was because the papers had written so much about him, and the reporters had built him up as a humane policeman who could understand everything.

"How long has it been," he asked, "since you wrote me the first letter?"

"It's more than two months. It was in a little café on Place du Tertre."

Maigret had been in the news a lot at the time, in connection with a crime committed by a young man of eighteen.

"So you wrote about ten letters, all of which you tore up? All in the space of about a week?"

"Yes, about that. I even used to write two or three the same evening and not tear them up till the next morning."

"Then for five or six weeks you came each Saturday to the Quai des Orfèvres?"

From the way he gave his name, waited in the glass cage, and then disappeared before he could be seen, he had become a fixture, like the madwoman and her knitting. Was it Janvier or Lucas who had christened him "the Saturday caller"?

Yet, during all this time Planchon had not acted on his threat. He had gone back each night to Rue Tholozé, lain down on his cot, got up first in the morning, and went on with his work as if nothing had happened.

Yet the man's mind was more subtle than one might think.

"I can guess what you're thinking," he murmured sadly.

"What's that?"

"That I've accepted the situation for almost two years. That, for two months, I've been talking about killing my wife or killing the pair of them."

"Well?"

"But I haven't done it yet. Admit that's it! You're thinking I'd never have the courage."

Maigret shook his head.

"That doesn't take courage. Any fool can commit murder."

"But what if there's no other way out? Put yourself in my place. I had a nice little business and a wife and a child. It's all being taken away from me. Not only my wife and child, but also my livelihood. Because they never discuss going away. In their eyes, I'm the one who's in the way, so it's up to me to go. That's what I'm trying to make you understand.

"Even the customers. It's happened gradually. Prou was just one of my employees, an intelligent, hard-working employee, I grant you. But he's got more small talk than I have. He handles the customers better than I do, especially the women.

"Without realizing it, he began to act as boss. When people called about a job, they nearly always asked for him. If I disappeared tomorrow, my absence would hardly be noticed. It's possible my daughter would be the only one who'd ask about me. And maybe not. He's more cheerful than I am. He tells her stories, sings songs for her, and takes her for rides."

"What does you daughter call him?"

"She calls him Roger, like my wife. It doesn't surprise her that they sleep in the same room. During the day, the cot's folded up and pushed into a closet; it's as if all trace of me was wiped out. . . . But I've kept you too long already. I'd like to apologize to your wife. She must be cross with me."

This time, it was Maigret, intent on understanding, who kept him from going.

"Listen to me, Monsieur Planchon . . ."

"Yes?"

"For two months, you've been trying to come to me and say, in so many words: 'I intend to kill my wife and her lover.' That's right, isn't it?"

"Yes."

"For two months, you've been living daily with this thought."

"Yes. There's nothing else I . . ."

"Just a moment! I don't suppose you expect me to say: 'Go ahead!' "

"You have no right to."

"But you think I should share your point of view?"

A quick flash in the man's eyes told him that he was not far from the truth.

"It's one of two things. Forgive me if I'm brutal with you. Either you have no intention of killing anyone—only the desire, especially after a few drinks . . ."

Planchon shook his head sadly.

"Let me finish. Or else, it seems to me, you haven't really made up your mind, and you want to find someone to dissuade you."

The man came back again with his eternal argument:

"There's no alternative."

"Did you expect me to find a solution for you?"

"There isn't one."

"Well now, suppose my theory's wrong. I can see only one other. You really have planned to kill your wife and her lover. You've even gone so far as to think of a place where you could get rid of the bodies."

"I've thought of everything."

"Yet you've come to see me, and my job is to lay my hands on criminals. . . ."

"I know."

"What do you know?"

"That it doesn't make sense."

His stubborn expression indicated that he was sticking to his story. He had started off in life without money, without means, with hardly any education. As far as Maigret could tell, his intelligence was fairly low.

Yet, though he had been left alone in Paris after his mother's death, he had managed, through sheer persistence, to become the boss of a small but prosperous business.

Could it be said that this man lacked logic? Even if he *had* started to drink?

"You mentioned confession. You said that, if you had continued to practice your religion, you would have gone and confided in a priest."

"I think so."

"What do you think the priest would have told you?"

"I don't know. I suppose he would have tried to persuade me to drop my plan."

"And what about me?"

"You, too."

"In other words, you want somebody to restrain you, to stop you from making a fool of yourself."

Planchon suddenly seemed lost. A moment earlier, he had been looking at Maigret with confidence, with hope. Suddenly, it was as if they were no longer talking the same language, as if all the words they had exchanged had been pointless.

He shook his head, and there was a sort of reproach in his eyes. Disappointment, anyway. He muttered very quietly:

"It's not that."

Was he on the point of taking his hat and leaving, sorry he had wasted his time coming?

"Look, Planchon. Try to listen to me, instead of following your own train of thought."

"I am trying, Monsieur Maigret."

"What benefit, what comfort would your confession to a priest have given you?"

He replied, still in a whisper:

"I don't know."

He was still only half there. He had begun to withdraw

29

into his shell, and to hear the chief inspector's voice only as he heard those anonymous voices in the evenings when he was propping up bars.

"Would you still have killed, afterward?"

"I suppose so. . . . It's time I went away."

Maigret, annoyed at disappointing him, kept on, searching for a glimmer of truth, which he thought, at times, he could perceive.

"You don't like being stopped from doing what you've decided?"

"No."

He added, with an odd smile:

"Unless I'm put in prison, it isn't possible. And so long as I haven't done anything, I can't be put in prison."

"So what you came here for was a kind of absolution? You had to know that you would be understood, that you weren't a monster, and that your plan was the only solution left to you."

Planchon repeated:

"I don't know."

He was so lost somewhere that Maigret felt like shaking him, yelling at him, staring him in the face.

"Look, Planchon . . ."

He was saying the same things, too, repeating himself.

"As you've just said, I have no right to lock you up. But I can have you watched, even if it doesn't prevent anything. You'd be arrested immediately. But it won't be me who tries you; it will be a court, and the prosecutors won't necessarily try to understand. They may be chiefly concerned with pre-meditation.

"Didn't you tell me that you had no family in Paris?"

"I haven't any anywhere."

"What will become of your daughter, even during the months while the case is being prepared? And afterward?"

Once again came the same old "I don't know."

"What will happen then?"

"I don't know."

"What are you going to do?"

"I have no idea. I'll try."

"Try what?"

"To get used to it."

Maigret felt like yelling at him that this was not what he was suggesting.

"What is there to stop you from leaving?"

"With my daughter?"

"You're still head of the family."

"What about her?"

"Is it your wife you're thinking of?"

Planchon nodded, ashamed: Then he added:

"And what about my business?"

This showed that it wasn't just a question of his feelings.

"Will you come back and see me?"

"I've told you everything. I've taken up too much of your time as it is. Your wife . . ."

"Never mind my wife. This concerns you. All right, don't come back and see me. But I want you to keep in touch. Don't forget it was *you* who came to see *me*."

"I'm sorry."

"You're to telephone me every day."

"Here?"

"Here or at my office. All I ask you to do is call me."

"Why?"

"No special reason. To keep in touch. You'll say: 'It's me!' And that will be enough."

"I'll do it."

"Every day?"

"Every day."

31

"And if, at some point, you feel you're about to put your plan into action, will you call me?"

He hesitated, seemingly weighing the pros and cons.

"That would mean that I wouldn't do it," he finally got out.

He was haggling, like a peasant at a market.

"You realize that if I call you to say that . . ."

"Answer my question."

"I'll try."

"That's all I'm asking. Now, go home."

"Not yet."

"Why not?"

"It's not time. They'll both still be in the dining room. What would I do?"

"Are you going to hang around in bistros again?"

He gave a resigned shrug and glanced at the decanter. Maigret, irritated, poured him a last glass.

"You might as well get drunk here as elsewhere."

The man hesitated, glass in hand, again ashamed.

"Do you despise me?"

"I don't despise anyone."

"But suppose you did despise someone?"

"It certainly wouldn't be you."

"Are you saying that to encourage me?"

"No. Because it's what I think."

"Thank you."

He rose and, holding his hat, glanced around as if looking for something else.

"I'd like you to explain to your wife . . ."

Maigret edged him gently toward the door.

"I've spoiled your evening. And hers, too."

He was on the landing now, more anonymous even than in Maigret's apartment, a small, very ordinary man whom no one would have looked at twice.

"Good-bye, Monsieur Maigret."

Phew! The door closed, and Madame Maigret shot out of the kitchen.

"I thought he'd never stop, and you'd never get rid of him. I almost came in to give you an excuse."

She stared at her husband.

"You seem preoccupied."

"I am."

"Is he mad?"

"I don't think so."

She rarely asked him questions. But this had happened at home. As she was bringing in the soup, she went so far as to murmur:

"What did he come for?"

"To confess."

She did not turn a hair, but sat down at the table.

"Aren't you going to switch on the television?"

"The programs must be nearly over."

In the old days, on Saturday evenings when he was not held up at the Quai des Orfèvres, they used to go to the cinema together, not so much for the entertainment as to be out together. They would stroll, arm in arm, toward Boulevard Bonne-Nouvelle. They felt at ease like that, with no need to talk.

"Tomorrow," said Maigret, "we'll go for a walk around Montmartre."

Arm in arm, like Sunday strollers. He wanted to see Rue Tholozé again, and look for a small house at the far end of a yard, where Léonard Planchon, his wife, his daughter, and Roger Prou lived.

Was he right? Was he wrong? Had he said the right things?

Had Planchon got what he was after in Boulevard Richard-Lenoir?

At that moment, he would be drinking somewhere, presumably thinking over all that had been said.

It was impossible to tell if this conversation, so much longed for and so often postponed, had brought him any relief, or if, on the contrary, it was going to start something.

It was the first time Maigret had said good-bye to a man on a landing of his home wondering if the same man might not, a little later, kill two people.

It could happen that very night, at any time, possibly at the very moment that Maigret was thinking about it.

"What's the matter?"

"Nothing. I don't like this business."

He thought of telephoning the police in the Eighteenth Arrondissement, to have a watch kept on Planchon's house. But how could you put a policeman on duty in the bedroom?

A policeman in the street would not be any use, either.

3

It was a typical Sunday morning, lazy, empty, and a bit dull. If Maigret happened to be at home on that day, he would stay in bed, even if he was not sleepy, knowing that his wife did not like him getting under her feet until she had done most of the housework.

He nearly always heard her get up quietly about seven o'clock. She would slip out of bed and cross to the door on tiptoe. Then he would hear the click of the switch in the next room, and a strip of light would appear at floor level.

He would go back to sleep again, without having really waked up. He knew that this was how things were supposed to be, and the knowledge entered his sleep.

Sunday-morning sleep was a different kind of sleep from that of other days. It had a different quality, and a different feel, too. For instance, every half hour, he would hear bells, and he would be aware of the emptiness of the streets, the absence of trucks and the fewer sounds of buses.

He also knew that he had no responsibilities. There was nothing hurrying him or waiting for him outside.

Later would come the muffled hum of the vacuum in the other rooms; later still, the smell of coffee, which he liked especially.

All families have their habits, traditions to which they cling. They provide color to even the gloomiest of days.

He dreamed of Planchon. It was not really a dream. He saw him, as he had on the previous day, in their small living room. But his attitude was different. Instead of being confused by emotion and despair, his features, disfigured by his harelip, conveyed irony and malice. Although the man was not moving his lips, Maigret had the impression that he was saying:

"Admit that you agree with me, that I have no alternative but to kill her. You don't dare to say it because you're an official, and you're afraid of doing the wrong thing. Yet you're not trying to restrain me. You're waiting for me to be done with her and with him. . . . "

A hand shook his shoulder gently and a familiar voice spoke the ritual words:

"It's nine o'clock."

His wife handed his his first cup of coffee, which he always drank before he got up.

"What's the weather like?"

"Cold. And windy."

Already washed and neat, wearing a pale-blue housedress, she opened the curtains. The sky was white, and the air looked white, too, icy white.

Maigret, in his dressing gown and slippers, went and sat down in the dining room, which had already been cleaned. The morning would now consist of certain rites that had gradually been established over the years.

Presumably it was the same in the apartments he could see on the opposite side of Boulevard Richard-Lenoir, as well as in most homes in Paris and elsewhere. Presumably these little humdrum habits answered some need.

"What are you thinking about?" his wife asked.

She had noticed that he was preoccupied, almost sullen.

"About that fellow yesterday."

Planchon's wife did not wake up her husband with hot coffee. When he opened his eyes, after a drunkard's restless sleep, he found himself on a folding cot in the dining room, and he was the one who got up first, hearing regular breathing from the next room, perhaps, and imagining two warm and relaxed bodies drowsing in his bed.

This picture affected him more than his visitor's long speech of the previous day had. Planchon had really only mentioned weekdays. But what happened on Sundays? His employees would not be waiting for him in the yard. He had nothing to do, either. It was probably Renée and her lover who were sleeping late at his place.

Did Planchon make coffee for them all, and set the table in the kitchen? Did his daughter, in her nightdress, barefoot, her face puffy with sleep, come and join him there?

The man had told him that she did not ask any questions, but that would not have stopped Isabelle from keeping her eyes open and wondering. What impression did she have of family life and of her father's?

Maigret ate his croissants while Madame Maigret began to get Sunday dinner ready. Now and then, they exchanged a few words through the kitchen door. The evening papers, which they had not read the day before, were on the table, with the weeklies, which he kept for Sunday mornings.

Another tradition was a telephone call to the PJ. Only, feeling slightly worried, he may have made it a little earlier.

Torrence was on duty. He recognized his voice, and imagined him in the near-empty offices.

"Anything new?"

"Nothing special, Chief. Except there was another jewel robbery last night."

"At the Crillon again?"

"At the Plaza-Athénée, on Avenue Montaigne."

Yet he had posted an inspector in each of the big hotels in the Champs-Elysées and in the surrounding area.

"Who was there?"

"Vacher."

"Didn't he see anything?"

"No. The same technique again."

Naturally, they had studied the records, including Interpol's, of all known jewel thieves. But this one's methods didn't tally with any of the others, and he was working nonstop, as if, in the space of a few days, he wanted to pile up a big enough fortune to retire on.

"Did you send someone to help Vacher?"

"Dupeu's gone to join him. There's nothing they can do right now. Most of the guests are still asleep."

Torrence must have found the next question an odd one.

"No incidents in the Eighteenth Arrondissement?"

"Nothing I can recall. Hang on while I look at the reports. Just a moment. *Bercy* . . . *Bercy* . . . I'll skip all the *Bercy's*. . . ."

These, in police jargon, were the drunk and disorderly who were hauled off to spend the rest of the night in a station lockup.

"A fight at 3:15 A.M. in Place Pigalle . . . Robbery . . . Another robbery . . . Stabbing, after a dance, in Boulevard Rochechouart."

A normal Saturday-evening tally.

"No murders?"

"I don't see any."

"Thanks. Give me a call if there's any news from the Plaza."

As he hung up, Madame Maigret asked him from the doorway:

"Are you worrying about that fellow yesterday?"

He looked at her like a man lost for an answer.

"Do you think he'll kill them in the end?" she said.

As he was going to bed last night, he had told his wife about Planchon's confession, lightheartedly, as if he did not take the matter seriously.

"You don't think he's off his head?"

"I don't know. I'm not a psychiatrist."

"Why do you think he came to see you? As soon as I saw him on the landing, I knew it wasn't an ordinary visit. I must admit he frightened me."

Why should he worry? Was it any of his business? Not yet, anyway. He answered his wife evasively, settled down in his armchair, and buried himself in the papers.

He had been sitting down only ten minutes when he got up and fetched the telephone directory. He found the name Planchon, Léonard, painter and decorator, Rue Tholozé.

The man had not lied about his identity. Maigret hesitated a moment before dialing the number, but finally did it. As the ringing echoed in a strange house, he felt something tighten in his chest.

At first he thought there was no one there, because the ringing went on a long time. Finally, there was a click, and a voice asked:

"What is it?"

It was the voice of a woman, and did not sound like she was in a very good mood.

"I'd like to speak to Monsieur Planchon."

"He's not here."

"Is this Madame Planchon?"

"It is, yes."

"Do you know when your husband will be back?"

"He's just gone out with his daughter."

Maigret noticed that she had said *his* daughter, and not *my* daughter or *our* daughter. He also realized that someone in the room was talking to the woman, presumably saying:

"Ask him his name."

In fact, after a short pause, she inquired:

"Who is this?"

"A customer. I'll call back."

He hung up. Renée was alive, all right. Roger Prou was, too, presumably, and Planchon had gone out with his daughter, which proved that Rue Tholozé, like other places, had its Sunday rites.

He hardly gave it another thought all morning. Once he had scanned the papers, with little interest, he stood for a while by the window, watching people coming back from Mass, walking briskly, leaning forward, their faces blue with cold. Then he had a bath and got dressed, as the smell of cooking spread into every corner of the apartment.

At midday, they ate, facing each other, because they were not watching television. They talked about Doctor Pardon's daughter, who was expecting her second child, and then about other things, which did not stick in his mind.

About three o'clock, the dishes washed and everything straightened up again, he suggested:

"How about a walk?"

Madame Maigret put on her astrakhan coat. He chose his thickest scarf.

"Where do you want to go?"

"To Montmartre."

"That's right. You said so yesterday. Shall we take the Métro?"

"It'll be warmer."

They got out at Place Blanche and began to walk slowly up Rue Lepic. The shutters of the shops there were closed.

Rue Lepic makes a large bend to the left where it meets Rue des Abbesses, and straight ahead Rue Tholozé climbs up a steep slope, and rejoins Lepic by the Moulin de la Galette.

"Is this where he lives?"

"A little farther up. At the foot of the steps."

Almost halfway up on the left, Maigret noticed a building with violet letters that lit up at night: BAL DES COPAINS. Three youths were standing on the sidewalk, apparently waiting for someone. From inside came the sound of an accordion. No one was dancing yet. The accordionist, at the end of the nearly dark room, was rehearsing.

It was here that, nine years before, the lonely Planchon had accidentally met Renée, because there was a crowd, and a harassed waiter had sat the the young girl down at his table.

The Maigrets, slightly out of breath, continued walking. Among five- or six-story apartment buildings were still a few low houses, which went back to the time when Montmartre was a village.

They came to an iron gate opening on a cobbled yard, at the end of which was a small stone house, the kind seen in the suburbs. It was one story, unusually dingy, and old-fashioned, with alternating red and yellow bricks around the windows. The woodwork was freshly painted blue, which clashed with the rest.

"Is this where he lives?"

They didn't dare stop, but merely took in as much as they could as they walked slowly by. Madame Maigret later remembered that the curtains were very clean. Whereas Maigret noticed the ladders in the yard, a handcart, and a wooden shed. Through its windows drums of paint were visible.

The van was not in the yard, and there was no garage. The curtains did not move. There was no sign of life. Were they to assume that Planchon, his wife, Isabelle, and Prou had all gone out together for a car-ride?

"What shall we do?"

Maigret did not know. He had had the urge to see, and now he had seen; he had no plan.

"Why don't we go up to Place du Tertre while we're here?"

They drank a carafe of vin rosé, and a long-haired artist offered to do their portraits.

The Maigrets were home by 6:00 P.M. He rang the Quai des Orfèvres. Dupeu was back. He had not found out anything at the Plaza. Some of the guests, who had spent the night out, had not yet rung for their breakfast.

He did not miss his television tonight, although there was a thriller on, which made him grumble all evening.

Although he enjoyed the boredom of Sunday, he enjoyed still more the moment, on Monday morning, when he took charge of his office again. He checked in and shook hands with his colleagues.

They discussed current cases, but Maigret preferred to keep quiet about the visit he had had on Saturday evening. Was he afraid he would seem absurd because he attached importance to it?

It was the only day of the week on which everyone shook hands. Lucas, Janvier, young Lapointe, and all the rest were there, except those who had been on night or weekend duty. All of them had, like himself, spent Sunday at home.

At last he picked Lapointe and Janvier and took them into his office.

"Have you kept the cards we made for the Rémond affair?"

This went back several months, to early autumn. It had been a question of collecting evidence against a man named Rémond who had many aliases and was suspected of having pulled off swindles in most of the countries of Europe. He lived in a furnished apartment in Rue de Ponthieu, and to get into it without arousing the owner's suspicions, Janvier and

42

Lapointe had turned up one morning with some official-looking cards from a fictitious office for revaluating building space.

"We have to measure every room, every hall," they had told the man.

They had briefcases stuffed with papers under their arms. Young Lapointe took notes solemnly while Janvier unrolled his steel tape measure and called off figures.

It was not entirely legal; still, it was not the first time they had used the trick, and it would serve again.

"Go to Rue Tholozé. At the very top, on the right, there's a small house at the far end of a yard."

Maigret would have given a lot to go there himself and sniff around this house about which he wanted to know everything.

He gave detailed instructions. Then, once his inspectors had gone, settled down to routine business.

The sky was still white and hard, and the Seine was a nasty gray. It was nearly midday before Janvier and Lapointe returned. Maigret took his time signing some official papers before he rang for Joseph to go and get them.

"Well?"

It was Janvier who spoke.

"We rang."

"Naturally. And it was the woman who opened the door. What was she like?"

They exchanged a glance.

"Dark, quite tall, good figure."

"Attractive?"

This time Lapointe chipped in:

"I'd describe her as a handsome female. A female more than woman."

"How was she dressed?"

"She was wearing a red dressing gown and slippers. She hadn't done her hair. She had a yellow nightdress on under the dressing gown."

"Did you see her daughter?"

"No. She must have been at school?"

"Was the van in the yard?"

"No. And there wasn't anyone in the shed."

"How did she react?"

"With suspicion. First, she looked at us through the curtains. Then we heard footsteps in the hall. She half opened the door and, showing only part of her face, asked: 'What is it? I don't want anything.'

"We explained what it was all about."

"Wasn't she surprised?"

"She asked: 'Are you doing this for the whole street?'

"When we answered yes, she decided to let us in.

" 'Will it take long?'

" 'Half an hour at the most.'

" 'Do you have to measure the whole house?' "

Then the two inspectors summed up their impressions. It was the kitchen that had struck them most.

"A wonderful kitchen, Chief, very bright and modern, with all the right equipment. You wouldn't expect to find a kitchen like that in an old house. There was even a dishwasher."

Maigret was not surprised. Wouldn't it be typical of Planchon to provide his wife with every comfort?

"In fact, it's a very cheerful house. You can see right away it belongs to a decorator, because everything seems to have been freshly painted. In the girl's bedroom, the furniture's been painted pink."

This detail, too, was typical of the Saturday caller.

"Go on."

"Next to the kitchen is a fairly big living room, which is used as a dining room, too, with country furniture."

"Did you find the folding cot?"

"In the closet, yes."

Janvier added:

"I remarked, casually: 'That's handy for putting up friends.' "

"She didn't react?"

"No. She followed us everywhere, watching what we did, not too convinced that we'd really been sent by an official agency. At one point, she asked: 'What's the point of all these measurements you're taking?'

"I handed her the blarney: that, now and then, because of alterations to buildings, we had to revise the bases for the property tax, and that, if they hadn't added anything on, they stood to gain by it.

"I don't think she's very bright, but she's not the sort of woman who's taken in easily, and I could see the moment coming when she'd pick up the phone and call our imaginary office.

"That was why we got through it as quickly as possible. There are two other rooms on the ground floor: a bedroom and a smaller room, which is used as an office and where the phone is.

"The bedroom, which is cheerful, too, hadn't yet been done up. The office was a typical small-business office: a few files, bills stuck on a hook, a twenty-four-hour stove, and samples blocking the fireplace.

"The bathroom isn't on the ground floor, but on the next floor, next to the girl's bedroom."

"Is that all?"

Lapointe joined in:

"There was a phone call while we were there. She made

the caller repeat the name twice, wrote it down on a notepad, and said: 'No, he's not here at the moment. He's out on a job. . . . What? Monsieur Prou, yes. I'll give him your message, and he'll come and see you, this afternoon, probably."

"Now, Chief, if you want to know the size of each room . . ."

They had done their job. Though Maigret was not much more enlightened, at least he had a clearer idea of the house, and it was just as he had imagined it.

Did the two men, the husband and the lover, work at the same place, or did they prefer to work on different jobs? Didn't they have to talk to each other àbout their work? What tone did they use?

Maigret went home for lunch and asked if anyone had called him. No, they had not, and it was not until just after six that the call he was expecting was put through to his office.

"Hello! Monsieur Maigret?"

"Yes."

"It's Planchon."

"Where are you?"

"In a café on Place des Abbesses, near a house where I've been working all day. I've kept my word. You asked me to call you."

"How do you feel?"

There was a pause.

"Do you feel calm?"

"I always feel calm. I've been thinking a lot."

"You went for a walk with your daughter yesterday morning, didn't you?"

"How did you know? I took her to the Flea Market."

"And in the afternoon?"

"They took the van."

"All three of them?"

"Yes."

"Did you stay at home?"

"I had a sleep."

So he was in the house when Maigret and his wife were passing the gate.

"I've been thinking a lot."

"What conclusions have you come to?"

"I don't know. There aren't any. I'm going to try to hang on as long as possible. Deep down, I wonder if I really want a change. And, as you said yesterday, I might lose Isabelle."

Maigret could hear the clink of glasses, a distant murmur of voices, and the ring of a cash register.

"Will you call me tomorrow?"

The man at the other end of the line hesitated.

"Do you think there's any point?"

"I'd rather you called me every day."

"Don't you trust me?"

How could he answer that question?

"I'll hang on; don't worry!"

He gave a sad little laugh.

"I've stuck it out for two years. And I'm enough of a coward to go on indefinitely. Because I *am* a coward, aren't I? Admit that's what you're thinking. Instead of doing something about it, like a man, I came sniveling to you."

"You had reason to come, and you didn't snivel."

"You don't despise me?"

"No."

"Did you tell your wife all about me, after I'd gone?"

"No. I didn't."

"Didn't she want to know who that maniac was who spoiled your supper?"

"You ask too many questions, Monsieur Planchon. You're too self-conscious."

"I'm sorry."

"Go home now."

"Home?"

Maigret was at a loss to know what to say to him. He didn't remember ever having been so embarrassed in his life.

"Well, it's *your* house, isn't it? If you don't want to go back there, go somewhere else. But do stop hanging around in bistros, because you'll only get more and more worked up."

"I feel you're annoyed."

"I'm not annoyed. I merely want you to stop chewing over the same ideas again and again."

Maigret was annoyed with himself. Had he been wrong to speak like that? It's difficult, especially on the telephone, to find the right words to say to a man who is planning to kill his wife and his co-worker.

It was an absurd situation and, to crown it all, it was as if Planchon had feelers. Though Maigret was not really annoyed, he resented being saddled with this affair, which he did not dare tell his colleagues about for fear they would think him a fool.

"Keep calm, Monsieur Planchon."

He could find only the stupid sort of formulas you use to comfort people.

"Don't forget to call me tomorrow. And keep telling yourself that what you have in mind won't settle anything. Quite the contrary."

"Thank you."

It was not convincing. Planchon was disappointed. He had just left work, and presumably had not yet drunk enough for it to make any difference or for him to see things a certain way, as on Saturday evening, for instance.

He must have been cold sober and without illusions. How did he see himself, in the absurd or loathsome role he was playing in his own home?

His "Thank you" had been bitter. Maigret wanted to go on talking, but he couldn't because his caller had hung up.

There was another solution, which the man had scarcely mentioned on Saturday, and which suddenly worried the chief inspector.

Now that Planchon had defined his problems by telling them to someone, and now that he could not foster any more illusions about himself, might he not be tempted to settle things by doing away with himself?

If Maigret had known where he had called from, he would have phoned him back immediately. But what could he say?

Good God! He did not *have* to do anything. It was not his job to sort out people's lives, but to lay hands on those who had committed crimes.

He worked for another hour, almost savagely, at the jewel-robbery case, which would probably keep him busy for weeks. It seemed obvious that the thief had, on each occasion, been a guest at the hotel from which the jewels had disappeared. The thefts had taken place in four different hotels, at two- or three-day intervals.

It would seem simple enough to study the lists of guests in the hotels, and to lay hands on the man or men who showed up on all the lists. But this did not work. And little more was gained from descriptions supplied by the hotel staff.

Weeks? It might take months. And it was possible that the story might end in London, Cannes, or Rome, unless they found signs of the jewels at some dealer's in Antwerp or Amsterdam.

Yet this was less depressing than dealing with Planchon. Maigret went home by taxi, because it was late. He had dinner, watched the television, went to sleep, and was awakened by the familiar smell of coffee.

At the office, he growled:

"Get me the Eighteenth Arrondissement station. . . . Hello, is that you, Bernard? Anything interesting last night? . . . No? No murders? No missing persons? Look, would you keep a discreet watch on a small house at the top of Rue Tholozé, just below the steps. . . . Yes. Not a twenty-four-hour watch, of course. Only at night. Just a glance on each round. Check, for instance, that a painter's van is in the yard. Thanks. Oh, yes, if it's not there, call me at home. . . . Nothing special. Just an idea. You know how it is. Thanks, my friend."

Just another routine day: people to question, not only about the jewels, but about two or three matters of lesser importance.

From six o'clock on, he kept an ear out for the phone. It rang twice, but it was not Planchon. At half past six, he still had not telephoned; nor at seven. Maigret grew annoyed with himself for feeling anxious.

Nothing could have happened during the daytime. It seemed inconceivable, for instance, that Planchon could take advantage of his daughter's being at school and go back and kill his wife, and then wait for Prou to return and do away with him, too.

In fact, Maigret had not asked him what weapon he intended to use. Yet the decorater had told him that he had worked out his double crime down to the last detail.

He was unlikely to have a gun, and even if he had, it was hardly likely that he would use it. Men like him, and most manual workers, normally tend to use a tool with which they are familiar.

What tool would a painter . . . ?

He could not help laughing at himself when he thought of a paintbrush.

At quarter past seven, he still had not called, so Maigret went home. The telephone did not ring during supper or during the evening.

"Still thinking about him?" his wife asked.

"Not all the time. But he worries me."

"You told me once that people who talk a lot rarely do anything."

"Rarely, I agree. But it does happen."

"Have you caught a cold?"

"Maybe on Sunday, in Montmartre. Do I sound thick?"

She got him an aspirin, and he slept right through the night. When he woke up, he saw rain streaming down the windows.

He waited until ten before he phoned the Eighteenth.

"Bernard?"

"Yes, Chief."

"Nothing from Rue Tholozé?"

"No. The van hasn't left the yard."

It was only at seven that evening, still without news, that he made up his mind to telephone Rue Tholozé.

A man's voice, which he did not recognize, replied:

"Planchon? Yes, that's right. But he's not here. He won't be here this evening, either."

4

Maigret had the impression that the man had started to hang up, but that, at the last moment, he had hesitated, as if he were suspicious. So the chief inspector quickly asked:

"What about Madame Planchon?"

"She's gone out."

"Won't she be back this evening, either?"

"She should be back any minute. She's gone shopping in the neighborhood."

Another pause. The instrument was so sensitive that Maigret could hear Prou's breathing.

"What do you want her for? Who are you?" the man finally asked.

Maigret almost passed himself off as a customer, with some story or other. After a pause, he decided to hang up.

He had never seen the man to whom he had spoken. The little he knew about him was through Planchon, who had reason to be prejudiced.

Yet as soon as he heard the sound of his voice, Maigret

felt antipathetic toward Renée's lover, even resented him. His antipathy did not stem from the decorator's story. It was the voice itself, its drawling, aggressive tone. He would have sworn that right now Prou was glaring suspiciously at the telephone, and that he never answered questions directly.

He was a type of man Maigret knew well, one who isn't easily thrown, who leers at you, and who, at the first awkward question, knits his bushy eyebrows.

Did he, in fact, have bushy eyebrows? And hair growing low on his forehead?

Maigret sorted through his papers in a bad temper, and then, in line with his routine, called in Joseph.

"Is there anyone else for me?"

Then he poked his head into the duty office.

"If anyone wants me, I'll be at home."

Out on the quai, he had to open his umbrella, and on the platform of the bus, he was squeezed up against someone in a dripping raincoat.

Before he sat down to supper, he again called Rue Tholozé. He was in a bad mood with everything and everybody. He was annoyed with Planchon for coming and bothering him with his absurd, pathetic story; he was annoyed with Roger Prou, heaven knows why; and he was annoyed with himself. He was almost annoyed with his wife, who was eying him anxiously.

Was it a rule, at the other end, not to answer right away? It was as if the phone were ringing in a void. Then he remembered that it was in the office. They probably had their meals in the kitchen, not the dining room, so there was some distance to cover.

"Hello!"

Someone at last! A woman.

"Madame Planchon?"

"Yes. Who is it?"

53

She spoke naturally, in a rather serious but not unpleasant voice.

"I was hoping to speak to Léonard."

"He's not here."

"Do you know when he'll be back? I'm a friend of his."

Then, as with Prou, there was a silence. Was Roger Prou beside her? Were they exchanging looks?

"What friend?"

"You don't know me. I was supposed to be meeting him this evening."

"He went out."

"For long?"

"Yes."

"Can you tell me when he'll be back?"

"I've no idea."

"Is he in Paris?"

Another hesitation.

"If he isn't, he hasn't left me his address. Does he owe you money?"

Maigret hung up once again. Madame Maigret, who had been listening to what he was saying, asked, as she was serving the soup:

"Has he disappeared?"

"It looks like it."

"Do you think he's killed himself?"

He muttered:

"I don't think anything."

He could see his visitor once again in the living room, his knuckles white from gripping his fingers, his pale eyes fixed on him pleadingly.

Planchon had been drinking and was under a strain. He had talked a lot. Maigret had let himself get involved, yet there were scores of questions he should have asked and which he had not.

After eating, he called the PJ's General Information. It was the time when the men on duty ate a snack, one eye on their telephones. The man who answered had his mouth full.

"No, Chief. No suicides since I've been on. Wait; I'll look through today's reports. Just a moment. An old lady threw herself out a window on Boulévard Barbès. A corpse was taken out of the Seine, just before five o'clock, at Pont de Saint-Cloud. From its condition, it's been in the water a fortnight. I don't see anything else."

It was Wednesday evening. The next morning, in his office, Maigret started scribbling on a sheet of paper.

It was on Saturday evening that he'd found Léonard Planchon waiting at home, on Boulévard Richard-Lenoir.

On Sunday morning, he had telephoned Rue Tholozé for the first time, and Madame Planchon had said that her husband had just gone out with his daughter.

That was true; the decorator had later confirmed it. Isabelle and her father had gone off, hand in hand, to the Flea Market in Saint-Ouen.

In the afternoon of the same Sunday, Maigret and his wife had walked past the little house. The van had not been in the yard. There had been no one visible through the curtains, but he had found out later, again through Planchon, that he had been asleep in the house.

Monday morning: Janvier and Lapointe, using questionably legal means, had called at Rue Tholozé and, under Renée's suspicious gaze, had checked all the rooms, on the pretense of measuring them.

About six Planchon had telephoned him at the Quai des Orfèvres, from a café on Place des Abbesses, so he said. Apart from a murmur of voices and the clink of glasses, he could hear the ring of a cash register.

The fellow's last words had been:

"Thank you!"

He had not mentioned a trip, or suicide. It was on Saturday that he had made a vague reference to this solution, which he had rejected so as not to leave Isabelle in the hands of Renée and her lover.

Tuesday: no telephone call. To set his mind at rest, Maigret had asked the police in the Eighteenth to keep an eye on the house on Rue Tholozé at night. Not a constant watch. The police, during their rounds, merely glanced at it to make sure nothing unusual was going on and that the van was still in the yard. It was.

Finally, Wednesday: nothing; no call from Planchon. And when he himself had telephoned, about seven in the evening, Roger Prou had answered that the decorator would not be back that evening. He sounded vague, as if on his guard. Renée was not in the house just then, either.

But, as her lover had said, she was there an hour later, and he gathered from her answers that she did not expect to see her husband for a long while.

He attended the conference, as he did every morning, but still did not mention the case, which did not officially exist. Shortly after ten, he left the Police Judiciaire in an icy drizzle and took a taxi to Rue Tholozé.

He did not yet know what he was going to do. He had no definite plan.

"Shall I wait?" asked the driver.

He decided to pay him off, because there was a chance he might be there some while.

The van was not in the yard, but an employee in a white coverall spotted with paint was moving around in the shed. Maigret made his way toward the little house and rang the bell. A window opened on the second floor, just above his head, but he did not move. Then he heard footsteps on the stairs, the door half opened, as it had to Janvier and Lapointe, and he saw some untidy dark hair, an almost equally dark look, a chalk-white face, and a splash of red dressing gown.

"What is it?"

"I'd like to speak to you, Madame Planchon."

"What about?"

The door remained open about six inches.

"About your husband."

"He's not here."

"That's why I want to talk to you. Because I need to see him."

"What do you want him for?"

He eventually decided to say: "Police."

"Have you got a warrant?"

He showed her his identification. Her attitude changed. She opened the door wider and stood aside to let him pass.

"I'm sorry. I'm alone in the house, and there have been some mysterious phone calls the last few days."

She was watching him closely, wondering if perhaps he was the person who had telephoned.

"Come in. The house is still a mess."

She showed him into the living room. There was a vacuum in the middle of the carpet.

"What has my husband done?"

"I have to get in touch with him so I can ask him some questions."

"Has he been in a fight?"

She pointed to a chair. She hesitated to sit down herself and held her dressing gown tightly in front of her.

"Why do you ask that?"

"Because he spends his evenings and part of the night in bistros, and when he's been drinking, he tends to get violent."

"Has he ever struck you?"

"No. Anyway, I wouldn't have let him. But he has threatened me."

"Threatened you with what?"

"To have done with me. He didn't say how."

"Did this happen several times?"

"Several times, yes."

"Do you know where he is now?"

"I've no idea, and I don't want to know."

"When was the last time you saw him?"

She stopped to think for a moment.

"Let's see. Today's Thursday. Yesterday was Wednesday. The day before that, Tuesday. It was Monday evening."

"What time?"

"Late."

"You don't remember the exact time?"

"It must have been around midnight."

"Were you in bed?"

"Yes."

"Alone?"

"No. I don't need to lie to you. Everyone around here knows, and I may add that everyone approves of us, Roger and me. If my husband wasn't so stubborn, we'd have been married years ago."

"You mean you have a lover?"

Looking him straight in the eye, she answered, not without some pride:

"Yes."

"Has he been living in this house?"

"So? When a man like Planchon digs his toes in and refuses a divorce, you have to . . ."

"For long?"

"It'll soon be two years."

"Did your husband accept the situation?"

"He's only been my husband on paper for a long time now. He hasn't been a real man for years. I don't know what you want him for. It's no concern of mine what he does away from here. What I can safely say is that he's a drunk, and you can't expect anything of him. If it wasn't for Roger, the business would no longer exist."

"I'd like to get back to Monday evening. You slept in this bedroom?"

The door was half-open. On the bed was an orange comforter.

"Yes."

"With this man you call Roger?"

"Roger Prou, a good man, who doesn't drink and works hard."

She referred to him proudly, as if she would have flown at the throat of anyone who dared to malign him.

"Did your husband have supper with you?"

"No. He hadn't got back."

"Did that often happen?"

"Fairly often. I'm getting to know how drunkards act. For a while, they preserve a certain amount of self-respect and decency. Then finally they drink so much they stop feeling hungry, and they have a few drinks instead of meals."

"Had your husband gone that far?"

"Yes."

"Yet he went on working? Might he not have fallen off a ladder or scaffolding?"

"He didn't drink during the day, or hardly ever. As for his work, if we had had to rely on him . . ."

"You have a daughter, I believe?"

"How did you know? I suppose you've been questioning the concierge. I don't mind; we've nothing to hide. I have a daughter, yes. She'll soon be seven."

"So, on Monday, you had supper together, this Roger Prou, you, and your daughter?"

"Yes."

"In this room?"

"In the kitchen. I can't see that it matters. We nearly always have our meals in the kitchen. Is that a crime?"

She was puzzled by the line the questions were taking, and was beginning to get impatient.

"I take it your daughter went off to bed first?"

"Of course."

She was obviously surprised to find him so well informed. Was she now going to connect his visit with the two men who had come to measure the rooms of the small house?

However, she didn't lose her composure, but went on studying her visitor, never looking away. Suddenly she asked him a question.

"By the way, you wouldn't happen to be the famous Chief Inspector Maigret, would you?"

He nodded, and she frowned. It wouldn't be so unusual for an ordinary policeman, a local inspector, for instance, to come and make inquiries about her husband's actions and movements, considering the life that Planchon led in the evenings. But for Maigret, in person, to take the trouble . . .

"In that case, it must be important."

Then she said, with a touch of irony:

"You're not going to tell me he's killed someone!"

"Do you think he's capable of it?"

"He's capable of anything. When a man goes that far . . ."

"Was he armed?"

"I've never seen a gun in the house."

"Did he have any enemies?"

"I was his only enemy, as far as I know. At least, in his mind. He hated me. He insisted on staying here, under conditions no man would have accepted, out of pure spite. He ought to have understood, if only for his daughter's sake."

"Let's go back to Monday. What time did you and Roger Prou go to bed?"

"Let's see . . . I went to bed first."

"What time?"

"About ten. Roger was working in the office, making out the bills."

"Was he the one who kept the accounts and took care of money matters?"

"If he hadn't done it, no one would have, because my husband wasn't capable anymore. Then, too, he put enough of his own money into the business."

"You mean he and Planchon were in partnership?"

"Yes. Well, at first there was nothing in writing between them. But they did sign a paper about two weeks ago."

She broke off and went into the kitchen, where something was boiling on the stove, but came back almost immediately.

"What else do you want to know? I have my housework to do, lunch to cook. My daughter will be back from school soon."

"I'm afraid I'll have to keep you a moment or two longer."

"You still haven't told me what my husband's done."

"I hope your answers will help me to find him. If I've understood you, your lover put money into the business?"

"Every time there wasn't enough to pay the bills."

"And two weeks ago, they signed a paper? What sort of paper?"

"A paper saying that, on payment of a certain amount, Prou would become owner of the business."

"Do you know how much the amount was?"

"I typed the paper."

"Can you type?"

"Sort of. There's been an old typewriter in the office for years. Planchon bought it before I got pregnant, a few months after our marriage. I was bored. I wanted something to do. So I started typing the bills with two fingers, and then letters to customers and suppliers."

"Do you still do it?"

"When necessary."

"Have you got this paper?"

She stared at him.

"I wonder if you have the right to ask me. I even wonder if I have to answer you."

"You don't have to, for the time being."

"For the time being?"

"I can always call you into my office as a witness."

"As a witness to what?"

"Your husband's disappearance, shall we say?"

"It's not a disappearance."

"What is it, then?"

"He's gone away, that's all. He should have gone a long time ago."

Even so, she got up.

"I don't see why I should hide anything from you. If the paper interests you, I'll go and get it."

She went into the office. There was the sound of a drawer being opened, and she came back a few seconds later holding a sheet of paper. It was headed LÉONARD PLANCHON, PAINTER AND DECORATOR. The words had been typed with a purple ribbon, some of the letters were higgledy-piggledy, and there were wide gaps between some words.

I, the undersigned, Léonard Planchon, transfer to Roger Prou, on payment of a sum of thirty thousand new francs (30,000), my share in the decorating firm situated on Rue Tholozé in Paris, which I hold in conjunction with my wife, Renée, née Babaud.

This transfer includes the lease of the building, household goods and furniture, but excludes my personal possessions.

The document was dated December 28.

"Normally," Maigret remarked, looking up, "agreements of this kind are signed in the presence of a lawyer. Why didn't you do this?"

"Because there was no point in paying the fee. When people are honest . . ."

"Was your husband honest, then?"

"*We* were, anyway."

"This paper was signed three weeks ago. From that time, Planchon was out of the business. I wonder why he went on working for it."

"And why he went on living in this house when he had been finished with it for still longer?"

"In fact, he worked as an employee?"

"More or less."

"Was he paid?"

"I suppose so. That was up to Roger."

"Were the thirty thousand francs paid by check?"

"In bills."

"Here?"

"Not in the street, anyway."

"In front of witnesses?"

"All three of us were witnesses. Our private affairs have nothing to do with anyone else."

"Weren't there any conditions to this arrangement?"

The question seemed to give her pause, and she remained silent for a moment or two.

"There was one. But he hasn't obeyed it."

"What was that?"

"That he should go away and give me my divorce at last."

"Still, he's gone."

"It took three weeks!"

"Let's get back to Monday."

"Again? Is this going to take long?"

"I hope not. You were in bed. Prou came and joined you. Were you awake when he went to bed?"

"Yes."

"Did you look at the time?"

"If you must know, we had other things to do. . . ."

"Were you both asleep when your husband came in?"

"No."

"Did he open the door with his key?"

"Not with a pen, anyway."

"He could have been too drunk to open the door himself."

"He was drunk but he found the keyhole."

"Where did he normally sleep?"

"Here. On a cot."

She got up again, opened the closet, and showed him a folded cot.

"Was it already set up?"

"Yes. I fixed it myself before I went to bed, so he wouldn't bang around for half an hour."

"And he didn't go to bed on Monday?"

"No. We heard him go up to the next floor."

"To kiss his daughter?"

"He never kissed his daughter in that state."

"What did he go to do?"

"We were wondering. So we listened. He opened the closet on the landing, where his things were. Then he went into the little room we use as an attic, because there isn't one in this house. There was a noise on the stairs, and I had to stop Roger from going to see what was happening."

"What was happening?"

"He was bringing down his suitcases."

"How many suitcases?"

"Two. We only had two in the house, anyway, because we never really went anywhere."

"Didn't you speak to him? Didn't you see him go?"

"Yes. When he was back in the living room, I got up. I motioned to Roger to stay where he was, so as not to cause a scene."

"Weren't you afraid? You told me that when your husband had been drinking he was violent, and that once or twice he'd threatened you."

"Roger was in earshot."

"How did your last conversation go?"

"I could hear him talking to himself, through the door, and he seemed to be snickering. When I went in, he looked me up and down and started laughing."

"Was he very drunk?"

"Not the same as usual. He didn't make any threats. He didn't pretend to be sober. And he didn't cry, either. Do you see what I mean? He seemed pleased with himself. It was as if he was going to play a trick on us."

"Didn't he say anything?"

"The first thing he came out with was: 'There you are, my dear!'

"He showed me the two suitcases, proudly."

She never once took her eyes off Maigret, and he, in turn, was carefully watching for the slightest flicker on her face. She must have noticed, but it did not seem to worry her.

"Is that all?"

"No. He also mumbled some words that more or less amounted to: 'You can look in them to make sure I'm not taking anything that belongs to you.'

"He was swallowing half his words, as if he was talking to himself, rather than me."

"Did you say he seemed pleased with himself?"

"Yes. I keep telling you. As if he was playing some trick on us. I asked him: 'Where are you going?'

"And he swung his arm around so hard he nearly lost his balance.

" 'Have you got a taxi at the door?'

"He looked at me, snickered again, but didn't answer.

When he picked up the suitcases, I caught him by his coat.

" 'It's not all that important, but I have to have your address, for the divorce proceedings.' "

"What did he answer?"

"I can remember exactly, because I repeated what he said, a little later, to Roger: 'You'll get it, my love. Sooner than you think . . .' "

"Didn't he mention his daughter?"

"He didn't say anything else."

"Didn't he go and kiss her in her bed?"

"We would have heard him, because Isabelle's room is right over our heads, and the floorboards creak."

"So he went to the door with two suitcases. Were they heavy?"

"I didn't pick them up. Quite heavy, but not all that much because he only took his clothes and his toilet things."

"Did you go with him to the door?"

"No."

"Why not?"

"Because it would have looked as if I was kicking him out."

"Did you see him cross the yard?"

"The shutters were closed. All I did, a little later, was go and bolt the front door."

"Weren't you afraid he'd go off with the van?"

"I would have heard the sound of the engine."

"Didn't you hear the sound of any engine? Wasn't there a taxi at the curb?"

"I have no idea. I was too delighted to know he was out of the house at last. I ran into the bedroom, and, if you must know the whole story, I flung myself into Roger's arms. He had got up and had heard everything through the door."

"That happened on Monday evening, didn't it?"

"Yes, Monday."

It was only on Tuesday that Maigret had asked the police in the Eighteenth to keep a discreet watch on the little house. According to Renée Planchon, it was too late.

"You have no idea where he could have gone?"

Maigret imagined he could again hear the last words Planchon had spoken to him over the telephone that same Monday, about six in the evening, from a bistro on Place des Abbesses.

"Thank you!"

He had felt, at that time, that the man's voice held a touch of bitterness, or slight irony.

If he had known where to call him, he would have done so immediately.

"Didn't your husband have any relations in Paris?"

"Neither in Paris nor anywhere else. I know that, because his mother was from the same village as mine—Saint-Sauveur, in the Vendée."

She obviously did not know that Planchon had seen Maigret and had confided in him. Yet everything she said confirmed what the chief inspector already knew.

"Do you think he's gone back there?"

"What for? He'd hardly know the place. He only went there two or three times with his mother when he was little, and if there's any family left, they're vague cousins, who've never shown any interest in him."

"You don't know if he has any friends?"

"Even when he was still all right, he was so shy and backward that I still wonder how he ever came to speak to me."

Maigret tried a little experiment.

"Where did you first meet him?"

"A little way down the street, at the Bal des Copains. I'd never set foot in it before. I'd just arrived in Paris, but I was working nearby. . . . I should have been on my guard against . . ."

"Against what?"

"A man who had something wrong with him."

"What had that to do with his character?"

"I don't know. But I understand it. People like that think about it the whole time; they feel different from others. They believe that everyone's looking at them and laughing at them. They're more sensitive. They're envious, bitter. . . ."

"Was he already bitter when you married him?"

"I didn't notice it right away."

"How long after?"

"I don't remember. He didn't want to see anyone. We hardly ever went out. We lived here like prisoners. He liked that. He was happy."

She stopped and looked at him as if to say they'd talked enough.

"Is that all?" she asked.

"That's all for now. I'd be obliged if you'd let me know as soon as you have any news. I'll leave you my phone number."

She took the card he handed her and put it on the table.

"My daughter will be back in a few minutes."

"Wasn't she surprised when her father went?"

"I told her he was on a trip."

As she showed him to the door, Maigret felt that she was worried and now wanted to delay him to ask some questions. But what?

"Good-bye, Chief Inspector."

He didn't feel too satisfied, either. Hands in his pockets and coat collar up, he went back down Rue Tholozé, passing a small girl with fair, tight pigtails. He turned to watch her and saw her go into the yard.

He would have liked to ask Isabelle some questions, too.

5

Planchon's wife had not asked him to take off his coat, so Maigret had remained nearly an hour bundled up in the overheated house. Out now in the fine drizzle, which seemed to be composed of invisible ice crystals, the cold gripped him. Ever since his Sunday walk in this district, he had felt a cold coming on. Now, this gave him the idea of turning left toward Place des Abbesses, instead of going down Rue Lepic to find a taxi on Place Blanche.

This was toward where the decorator had telephoned him from on Monday evening. It was the last time they had been in touch.

Place des Abbesses, with its Métro station, the Théâtre de l'Atelier, which looked like a toy or a stage set, and its bistros and small shops, seemed to Maigret to be far more genuine working-class Montmartre than Place du Tertre, which had become a tourist trap. He remembered that when he had first discovered Place du Tertre, shortly after his arrival in Paris, one chilly morning in spring sunshine, he had felt that he had been transported into a picture by Utrillo.

The place, when he reached it, was swarming with ordinary people, people from the surrounding area, coming and going. It was like a big town on market day, and it was also as if there were some family link between all these people, as in a village.

He knew from experience that some of the older ones had never set foot outside the neighborhood, and that there were still shops that had been handed down from father to son for several generations.

He looked through the windows of several bistros before he noticed, on a tobacco counter in a café, a small cash register, which seemed new.

Remembering the noises he had heard during his conversation with Planchon, he went in.

It was nice and warm inside, with a homey smell of wine and cooking. The tables, seven or eight at the most, were covered with paper tablecloths, and a slate announced that there were sausages and mashed potatoes for lunch.

Two workmen in overalls were already eating at the far end. The proprietress, dressed in black, was sitting at a desk against a background of cigarettes, cigars, and lottery tickets. A man with his sleeves rolled up to the elbows, wearing a blue apron, was serving wine and apéritifs at the bar.

There were about ten people drinking, and they all turned to look at him. After a fairly long silence, they started talking again.

"A hot toddy," he ordered.

Madame Maigret had confirmed that his voice was a different pitch from normal. He would probably become hoarse.

"Lemon?"

"Yes, please."

At the far end, near the kitchen, he could see a telephone booth with a glass door.

"Excuse me. Do you have a customer with a harelip?"

He knew that his neighbors were listening, even those with their backs to him. He was almost sure they had guessed that he was from the police.

"A harelip," repeated the man in shirtsleeves. He had put the rum toddy down on the bar and was pouring wine from one bottle into another.

He paused before he replied, as if respecting a kind of solidarity.

"A small fellow. With fair, slightly reddish hair."

"What's he been up to?"

One of the customers, who looked like a salesman, broke in:

"Don't kid yourself, Jean! You don't think Chief Inspector Maigret's going to tell you."

There was a roar of laughter. They had not only guessed he was from the police, but also recognized him.

"He's disappeared," Maigret muttered.

"Popeye?"

Jean explained:

"We call him Popeye because we don't know his name, and he's like the cartoon character."

He raised his hand to his lips, as if to cut them in two, and added:

"The hole looked as if it had been specially made to stick a pipe in."

"Is he a regular?"

"Not really a regular, because we don't know who he is, or even if he's a local. But he used to come a lot. Almost every evening recently."

"Did he come in on Monday?"

"Today's Thursday. . . . On Tuesday, I went to see old Nana buried. She used to sell papers on the corner. Monday . . . Yes. He came in on Monday."

"He asked me for a token for the phone," broke in the proprietress from her desk.

"About six?"

"It was just before suppertime."

"Did he speak to anyone?"

"He never spoke to anyone. He used to stand at the end of the bar, about where you are, and order brandy. He would stand there, lost in his thoughts. They couldn't have been very cheerful ones, because he always looked depressed."

"Were there many people here on Monday evening?"

"Fewer than now. We don't serve meals in the evening. Some of the customers were playing belote at that table on the left."

It was the one where the two workmen were eating grilled sausages, which made the chief inspector's mouth water. Some dishes always seem better in restaurants, especially in small bistros, than at home.

"How many brandies did he drink?"

"Three or four. I can't remember exactly. Do you know, Mathilde?"

"Four."

"About his normal ration. He used to stay quite a while. Sometimes he'd turn up around nine or ten—in which case he wouldn't look too good. I suppose he'd been to other local bars."

"Did he ever join in the conversation?"

"Not that I know of. Did anyone ever speak to him?"

The salesman broke in again:

"I tried once, but he looked right through me. Mind you, he was well gone by then."

"Did he ever cause trouble?"

"He wasn't the type. The more he drank, the calmer he got. I swear I've seen him crying, all by himself, at his end of the bar."

Maigret had a second toddy.

"Who is he?" Jean asked.

"A painter-decorator, from Rue Tholozé."

"I told you he was a local," someone said. "Do you think he's committed suicide?"

Maigret did not think anything, especially now, after his long talk with Renée. As Janvier had said—or was it Lapointe?—she was more a female than a woman, a female who clings to her male and who will, if necessary, defend him ferociously.

She had not been flustered. She had answered all his questions. Though she had sometimes hesitated, it was because she was not very intelligent and was trying hard to grasp their meaning.

The less educated people are, the more suspicious they seem. She had not changed much since she had left her village in the Vendée.

"What do I owe you?"

When he left, they all looked after him, and they would no doubt start to talk about him almost before the door was shut. He was used to it. He found a taxi almost right away and went home.

He ate his roast veal without appetite, and his wife wondered why he suddenly said:

"Make some sausages tomorrow."

He was at the Quai des Orfèvres by two o'clock. Before going up to his office, he stopped to see the Hotels Squad.

"I want you to try to trace a certain Léonard Planchon, a decorator, thirty-five years old, living on Rue Tholozé. He may have moved into a hotel, probably a small one, also probably in the Montmartre area, with two suitcases, near midnight on Monday. He's on the small side, with fair, slightly reddish hair, and a harelip. . . ."

The squad would examine hotel registration forms and check boarding houses.

A few moments later, he was sitting at his desk, unable to decide which pipe to smoke. He called in Lucas.

"Circulate all taxi drivers. I want to know if any of them picked up a fare carrying two suitcases, on Monday around midnight, near Rue Lepic or Place Blanche."

He repeated the description, including, of course, the harelip.

"While you're at it, inform the railroad stations, just in case."

It was all routine, and Maigret did not seem to have much faith in it.

"Has your Saturday caller disappeared?"

"Looks like it."

Then he was so busy with other things that he didn't think about him for a whole hour. When he got up to switch on the lights, because the sky was growing darker and darker, he suddenly decided to go and see his boss, the director.

"I want to have a word with you about something that's on my mind."

He felt slightly ridiculous for attaching so much importance to it, and as he described the conversation he'd had at home on Saturday, he felt that his story was not very convincing.

"Are you sure he's not mad, or slightly unbalanced?"

The big chief also came across such people, because some of them, through obstinacy or cunning, managed to get to see him. Sometimes it was only at the end of a story that he realized it did not hold water.

"I don't know. I've seen his wife."

He summarized his morning conversation with Renée.

His boss, as he had expected, did not see things in the same light, and appeared surprised by Maigret's concern.

"Are you afraid he's committed suicide?"

"It's a possibility."

"You've just said that he talked to you about doing away with himself. What I can't understand, in that case, is why he took the trouble to go and get his things, and saddle himself with two suitcases."

Maigret sucked at his pipe, but did not say a word.

"Perhaps he wanted to get away from Paris. Perhaps he moved into the nearest hotel."

Maigret shook his head.

"I'd like to know more about it," he said with a sigh. "I wanted to get your permission to call the lover in to my office."

"What sort of man is he?"

"I haven't seen him, but from what I know, he can't be a very easy man. And there are the employees. I'd like to question them."

"In view of how things stand with the examining magistrates, I'd rather you had a word or two with the Public Prosecutor's Office."

The same old antagomism still existed, though fairly well disguised, between the Police Judiciaire and the gentlemen at the Palais de Justice. Maigret could remember the time when he could carry out an investigation without referring to anyone, and get in touch with an examining magistrate only after the matter had reached a satisfactory conclusion.

Since then there had been new laws and no end of decrees, and to keep on the right side of the law, you had to watch what you did. Even his morning visit to Rue Tholozé could, if Renée Planchon decided to make a complaint, bring severe censure.

"You don't want to wait for the result of further inquiries?"

"I have a feeling they aren't going to produce anything."

"Go ahead, if you must. I wish you good luck."

So it was that, about five o'clock in the afternoon, Maigret went through the little door that cuts off the Police Judiciaire from a very different world in the Palais de Justice.

On the other side were the public prosecutor, examining magistrates, judges, courtrooms, and vast corridors, with lawyers in black gowns who looked as if they were flapping their wings.

The prosecutors' offices were stately and opulent compared with those of the police. Strict etiquette was observed there and everyone seemed to speak in whispers.

"I'll show you in to Deputy Prosecutor Méchin. He's the only one free at the moment."

He waited a long while, just as others waited to see him in the glass cage at the PJ. Then a door opened into an Empire-style office, and he found himself walking on a red carpet.

Méchin was tall and fair, and his dark suit was immaculately cut.

"Please take a seat. What's the trouble?"

He glanced at the platinum watch on his wrist, like a man whose time is precious. He looked as if he ought to be sipping tea in some aristocratic drawing room.

It seemed vulgar, almost in bad taste, to bring up the little decorator from Rue Tholozé, his long story, interrupted two or three times to swallow some calvados, his tears and his passionate outbursts.

"I still don't know whether it's a simple disappearance, a suicide, or a crime."

He summed up the situation as best he could. The deputy prosecutor listened to him, studying his hands and their manicured nails. They were very fine hands, with long slender fingers.

"What do you intend to do?"

"I would like to hear what the lover, Roger Prou, has to

say. Possibly also the three or four employees at Rue Tholozé."

"Is he the kind of man who's likely to object, or be a nuisance?"

"I'm afraid so."

"Do you think it's necessary?"

The affair took on a different light here, even more than in his chief's office, and Maigret was tempted to give up and erase from his memory the little man with the harelip who had burst so indecently into his life on Boulevard Richard-Lenoir.

"What's in your mind?"

"Nothing. It's all in the air. I've got to see Prou to start me going in the right direction."

Then, when he had given up hope of getting consent, the deputy prosecutor glanced again at the time and got up.

"Serve him with a summons for questioning. But be careful. As for the employees, if you really must . . ."

A quarter of an hour later, Maigret was in his office filling in the spaces on an official form. Then he called Lucas.

"I'd like the names and addresses of the men employed by Planchon. You can ask the social security people. They must have the names in their files."

An hour later, he was filling in three other forms, because, in addition to Roger Prou, there were three employees, including an Italian named Angelo Massoletti.

After this, until nine in the evening, he heard witnesses in regard to the jewel thefts, especially staff members of the hotels where these thefts had been committed. He had some sandwiches sent in, went home at last, and drank another toddy, with two aspirin, before going to bed.

At nine o'clock the next morning, a well-built man with white hair and a fresh complexion was already in the waiting room, and, five minutes later, he was shown into Maigret's office.

"Is your name Jules Lavisse?"

"I'm known as Pépère. Some people call me St. Peter, because, I suppose, they think my white hair's a halo."

"Have a seat."

"Thanks. I'm more often up a ladder than on a chair."

"Have you been working for Léonard Planchon long?"

"I was working for him when he was still a youngster, and when the boss's name was Lempereur."

"So you know what's been going on on Rue Tholozé?"

"That depends."

"On what?"

"On what you do with what I say."

"I don't follow."

"If you want to mention it afterward to the boss's wife or Monsieur Roger, I just work there and I don't know anything. Especially if I have to repeat what I say in court."

"Why in court?"

"Because when you have people come here, it means that something funny's going on, doesn't it?"

"Do you think there's something funny going on on Rue Tholozé?"

"You haven't answered me."

"There's every chance that this conversation will remain within these four walls."

"What do you want to know?"

"How are things between your boss and his wife?"

"Didn't she tell you? I saw you crossing the yard yesterday, and you stayed over an hour with her."

"Has Prou been her lover long?"

"I don't know anything about him being her lover. But he's been sleeping in the house for two years."

"And how has Planchon taken it?"

The old housepainter gave a wry smile.

"Like a cuckold!"

"You mean he accepted the situation in good part?"

"Good part or not, he hadn't much choice."

"But it was his home."

"Maybe he thought it was his, but it was really hers."

"When he married her, she had nothing."

"I remember. It doesn't change the fact. As soon as I saw her, I knew he wouldn't have any more say in things."

"Do you think Planchon's a weak man?"

"In a way. I'd say more that he's a good man who's been unlucky. He could have been happy with any woman. And he had to pick that one."

"Yet they were happy for some years."

The old man shook his head doubtfully.

"I suppose so."

"You don't agree?"

"Maybe he was happy. Maybe she was happy, too. But they weren't happy together."

"Was she unfaithful to him?"

"I think she was unfaithful to him even before she moved to Rue Tholozé. Mind you, I didn't see her. But since she's been Madame Planchon . . ."

"With whom?"

"Anything in trousers. With nearly all the employees who worked there. If I'd been a bit younger . . ."

"Planchon didn't suspect anything?"

"Do husbands ever suspect anything?"

"How about Prou?"

"She ran into a tough customer there, a man with ideas. It wasn't enough for him to have his fun up against a wall, like the rest."

"Do you think he meant to take over from his boss from the beginning?"

"In his bed, first of all. Then as head of the business . . . Look, if you repeat what I'm telling you, I may just as well go and look for another job. Apart from which, he might be waiting for me one day around a corner."

"Does he get violent?"

"I've never seen him strike anyone, but I wouldn't like him for an enemy."

"When did you last see Planchon?"

"Well, we're there at last! You've taken your time. I had the answers all ready when I came, because I thought that would be the first thing you'd ask me. Monday, half past five."

"Where?"

"On Rue Tholozé. I wasn't on the same job. I had to repaint an old lady's kitchen on Rue Caulaincourt. The boss and the others were working on a new house on Avenue Junot. A big job. At least three weeks. I went to Rue Tholozé about half past five, as I told you, and I was in the shed when the van came back into the yard. The boss was driving, with Prou next to him, and Angelo and Big Jef behind."

"Did you notice anything special?"

"No. They unloaded some gear, and the boss, as usual, went into the house to change. He always changes after work."

"Do you know how he spent his evenings?"

"I sometimes used to run into him."

"Where?"

"In various bistros. Ever since Prou moved in, he's been boozing it up, especially in the evening."

"Have you ever thought he might commit suicide?"

"It never occurred to me."

"Why?"

"Because when you stick a situation like that for two years, there's no reason you shouldn't accept it the rest of your life."

"Did you ever hear that he wasn't the boss anymore?"

"He hadn't been for ages. They let him believe it, but in fact . . ."

"Did anyone tell you that Prou had bought the business?"

The man nicknamed Pépère stared at him out of his beady little eyes and shook his head.

"Did they get him to agree, to sign something?" he asked. Then, as if talking to himself, he said:

"They're even smarter than I thought."

"Didn't Prou mention it?"

"First I heard of it. It doesn't surprise me, though. Is that why he left? Have they finally thrown him out?"

The idea seemed to upset him.

"What I can't really understand is why he didn't take his daughter with him. I was convinced he was sticking it out for her sake."

"Did they say anything on Tuesday?"

"Prou told us that Planchon had left."

"He didn't tell you how and why?"

"Only that he was dead drunk when he came home and packed his things."

"Did you believe him?"

"Why not? Isn't that how it happened?"

A look of curiosity came into his eyes.

"You know something, don't you?"

"How about you?"

"I'm not that clever."

"Weren't you surprised?"

"I told my wife, when I got home that evening, that Planchon probably wouldn't last much longer. If anyone loved his wife, he did. To the point of being ridiculous. And his daughter—well, she was the world to him."

"Did you go in the van on Tuesday morning?"

"We all got in it. Prou drove. He dropped me off on Rue Caulaincourt, opposite my old lady."

"Did you notice anything out of the ordinary?"

"There were just the usual cans of paint, some rolls of wallpaper, some brushes and sponges, and all the rest of it."

"Thank you, Monsieur Lavisse."

"Is that all?"

The old man seemed disappointed.

"Would you like me to ask you some more questions?"

"No. I thought it would take longer, that's all. It's the first time I've been here."

"If you remember anything else, don't hesitate to come see me or telephone."

"Prou will ask me what we talked about."

"Tell him I checked up on Planchon, how he behaved, whether it's likely he committed suicide."

"Do you think it is?"

"I know no more than you."

Lavisse left, and a few moments later the young Italian, whose Christian name was Angelo, took his seat, which was still warm. He had been in France only six months, and Maigret was forced to repeat each question two or three times.

One of them seemed to surprise him:

"Has your boss's wife ever made advances to you?"

He was a good-looking young fellow, with soft, melting eyes.

"Advances?"

"Did she try to get you into the house?"

This made him laugh.

"And what about Monsieur Roger?" he objected.

"Is he jealous?"

"I think he . . ."

He went through the motions of sticking a dagger in his chest.

"Have you seen Monsieur Planchon since Monday?"

That was all for him. And the third employee, called for eleven o'clock, the one known as Big Jef, answered most of the questions by merely saying:

"I don't know."

He didn't want to get involved in other people's business, and he didn't seem to have any great affection for the police. Maigret found out later that he had been arrested two or three times for creating a disturbance, and once for assault and wounding, after breaking a bottle over the head of a nearby man in a bar.

Maigret had lunch at the Brasserie Dauphine with Lucas, though his inspector had nothing to report. The circular to the taxi drivers had produced nothing. This meant little, because some of them avoided contact with the police as much as they could. They were all well aware that it meant time wasted: interrogations at the Quai des Orfèvres, then with the examining magistrate, and finally, sometimes, two or three days of hanging around in the witnesses' anteroom at court.

Though the Hotels Squad was one of the most efficient, it had found no trace of Planchon. As far as could be judged, he was not the sort of man to obtain false papers. If he had landed at a hotel or boardinghouse, it would have been under his own name.

The last picture of him was that of a little man, weighed down with two suitcases, walking along Rue Tholozé near midnight. Of course, he might have taken a bus and gone to a station, where he would not necessarily have been noticed.

"What do you think of it, Chief?"

"He promised to phone me every day. He didn't on Sunday, but he called me on Monday."

He had not killed Renée and her lover. Had he decided to leave on the spur of the moment? About eight o'clock, he had left the bistro on Place des Abbesses, and by then he had already drunk several brandies. The chances were that he had been into several other drinking haunts. A thorough search of the neighborhood would no doubt reveal his tracks.

Once he was drunk, what ideas had passed through his head?

"If he threw himself in the Seine, it might be weeks before he's fished out," Lucas muttered.

It was obviously absurd to imagine the man with the harelip filling his suitcases with all his private belongings and lugging them through the streets just to go throw himself in the Seine.

Maigret, who was still nursing his cold, though it had not actually come into the open, had a brandy with his coffee. At two o'clock, he was back in his office.

Roger Prou made him wait a good ten minutes. So the chief inspector, in turn and as if in revenge, let him stew in the waiting room until quarter of three. Lucas went and had a look at him two or three times, through the glass.

"How does he seem?"

"Not easy."

"What's he doing?"

"He's reading the paper, but he keeps glancing at the door."

Joseph finally showed him in. Maigret remained seated, bent over his papers, which seemed to demand all his attention.

"Sit down," he growled, pointing to one of the chairs.

"I haven't all afternoon to waste."

"I'll be with you in a moment."

Even so, he went on reading, underlining certain phrases in red pencil. This took another ten minutes, after which Maigret got up, opened the door of the duty room, and spent some time muttering instructions.

Only then did he really look at the man sitting in one of the green velvet–upholstered chairs. He went back to his place at his desk. When he spoke, his voice was quite expressionless:

"Is your name Roger Prou?"

6

"Roger Etienne Ferdinand Prou," he answered, isolating the syllables. "Born in Paris, on Rue de la Roquette."

Half-rising from his chair, he pulled a wallet from his hip pocket and took from it an identity card. He laid it on the desk and said:

"No doubt you want proof."

He was freshly shaved and was wearing a blue suit, presumably the one he wore on Sundays. Maigret had not been far wrong in imagining him with very dark, wiry hair, growing low on his forehead, and bushy eyebrows.

He was a handsome male, in the same way that Renée was a handsome female. Their calm, yet aggressive, manner made one think of wild beasts. Though Prou had been abrupt on principle, because he was being made to waste his own and his employees' time, he was not being put off by the chief inspector's time-honored ploy. His expression was mainly ironical.

In the country, he would have been cock of the walk, the

one who, on Sundays, persuades his friends to go and antagonize the fellows of the neighboring village and who cynically puts girls in the family way.

In a factory, he would have been the troublemaker, crossing swords with the foreman and casually provoking incidents to establish prestige over his co-workers.

With his build and with the character Maigret suspected he had, he could have been a pimp, too. Not at the Etoile, but in the Porte Saint-Denis or Bastille areas. You could easily imagine him playing cards all day in cafés while keeping a sharp eye on the street.

He could even have been the leader of a gang, probably not a killer, but the organizer, for instance, of warehouse burglaries around the Gare du Nord or in neighboring suburbs.

Maigret pushed back his identity card, which was in order.

"Have you brought the paper I asked for?"

Prou had kept his wallet in his hand. With thick, confident fingers, he calmly pulled out the sheet of paper, signed Léonard Planchon, which made him co-owner, with his mistress, of the painting and decorating firm.

He handed it to the chief inspector with the same calm and disdain.

Maigret got up, went over again to the duty room, and stood in the doorway, in order not to lose sight of his visitor.

"Lapointe!"

Then he whispered:

"Take this up to Monsieur Pirouet. He knows about it."

This meant the Forensic Laboratory, up under the roof of the Palais de Justice. Pirouet, a comparatively recent acquisition to the PJ, was a curious fellow, fat and hearty. He'd been looked on with some mistrust when he came, as an assistant chemist, because he looked more like a salesman. The inspectors soon began referring to him, ironically, as Monsieur Pirouet, with the accent on the Monsieur.

Yet he had turned out to be a first-rate colleague, versatile and inventive; he'd already built several ingenious machines with his own hands. They'd also found out that he was an astonishingly good graphologist.

Before Prou's visit, Maigret had sent an inspector to the social security offices to obtain some pay slips with Planchon's signature on them. These had been sent upstairs.

It was a dull day. Fog was descending on the streets, as it had on the previous Saturday.

The chief inspector regained his seat, moving as if in slow motion. Prou, in spite of his apparent calm, spoke first:

"I take it you called me in to ask some questions?"

Maigret gave him an almost friendly look.

"Certainly," he murmured. "I still have some questions to ask, but I don't quite know what."

"I warn you that if you're making a fool of me . . ."

"I have no intention of making a fool of you. Your former boss, Planchon, has disappeared, and I would like to know what's become of him."

"Renée told you."

"She told me that he left on Monday with his two suitcases. You saw him go, too, didn't you?"

"Wait a minute! Don't go putting words in my mouth. I *heard* him. I was behind a door."

"So you didn't see him go?"

"Not quite. I heard them talking. I also heard him going upstairs to get his things. Then his footsteps in the hall and the front door shutting again. And then I heard his footsteps in the yard."

"Since then, he's vanished."

"How do you know? A man doesn't disappear just because he leaves home."

"It so happens that Planchon should have telephoned me on Tuesday."

Maigret had not planned his interrogation, and this apparently harmless remark was an inspiration of the moment. Naturally, he did not once take his eyes off the man facing him. Did Prou's reaction disappoint him? He definitely gave a slight start. His bushy eyebrows drew together. He seemed to grasp the situation in a matter of seconds, to understand all that these few words implied:

"How do you know he should have phoned?"

"Because he promised to."

"Did you know him?"

Maigret avoided answering and began filling a pipe with fussy little prods that would have driven anyone else mad. Yet Roger Prou gave no sign of nervousness.

"Let's talk about you. You're twenty-eight?"

"Twenty-nine."

"You were born on Rue de la Roquette. What was your father?"

"A carpenter. He had, still has, his workshop at the end of a cul-de-sac. Since you must know everything, he specializes in repairing antiques."

"Any brothers or sisters?"

"Sisters."

"So you were the only boy in the family. Didn't your father try to teach you his trade? It's a dying craft, I understand, and there's a good living to be made at it."

"I worked with him until I was sixteen."

He was purposely talking as if he were reciting a school lesson.

"After which?"

"I got fed up with it."

"You preferred being a housepainter?"

"Not right away. My aim was to be a professional bicycle racer. Not long-distance. Not the Tour de France. A track cyclist. I raced two years as a junior at the Vélodrome d'Hiver."

"Did that earn you enough to feed yourself?"

"No, it didn't. And when I realized I was too heavy, and that I'd never be a star, I gave it up. Do you want to know the rest?"

Maigret nodded, drew slowly on his pipe, and toyed with a pencil.

"I got my military-service call brought forward, so I could get it over with."

"You already had something in mind."

"Exactly. There's no reason why I shouldn't tell you. To earn enough money to be a free man."

"What did you do when you got back to Paris?"

"First I worked in a garage, but it was too boring for my taste. On top of which, I had a boss who was constantly breathing down my neck, and we more often used to work ten or twelve hours a day than eight. Then I was an apprentice locksmith for a few months. Finally, one of my friends got me into the painting-decorating business."

"With Planchon?"

"Not then. With Desjardins and Brosse, on Boulevard Rochechouart."

They were getting nearer Montmartre and Rue Tholozé.

"Were you saving any money?"

Prou got the message.

"Of course."

"Much?"

"As much as I could."

"When did you start with Planchon?"

"Just over two years ago. I had a fight with one of the bosses. Anyway, it was too big a business. I wanted to work for a small place."

"Were you still living with your parents?"

"I'd been living alone for some time."

"Where?"

"At the end of Rue Lepic. In the Hôtel Beauséjour."

"I suppose you met Planchon in a café, and he told you he was looking for a good worker?"

Prou again looked at him with a frown. Maigret was not surprised to discover that his reactions were almost identical to Renée's.

"What are you trying to make me say?"

"Nothing. I'm collecting facts. Planchon must have gone to the local bistros. It's only natural to assume . . ."

"You assume wrong."

"Of course you could have met Madame Planchon when she was doing her shopping or . . ."

"Is that why you're wasting my time, just to hand out all this chat?"

He looked as if he were going to get up and head for the door.

"For one thing, I didn't meet Renée before I went to work on Rue Tholozé. And for another, it wasn't her who put me on to her husband. All right?"

Maigret replied with an odd sort of a smile:

"All right. Did you answer an advertisement? Did you see a notice outside the gate asking for a worker?"

"There wasn't any notice. I stopped in on the off chance. And it so happened that just then they needed someone."

"How long afterward did you become Madame Planchon's lover?"

"Now look here, what right have you got to poke into people's private lives?"

"Planchon has disappeared."

"That's what you say."

"You don't have to answer."

"Suppose I don't?"

"I'll be free to draw my own conclusions."

Prou muttered disdainfully:

"About a week."

"In fact, it was love at first sight?"

"She and I clicked right away."

"Did you know that she had also clicked, as you put it, with most of your friends?"

At this, Prou's face turned red and he clenched his teeth.

"Did you know?" Maigret repeated.

"That's nothing to do with you."

"Do you love her?"

"That's my business."

"How long was it before Planchon caught you?"

"He didn't catch us."

Maigret feigned surprise.

"I thought he caught you red-handed, and, as a result, that . . ."

"That what?"

"Just a minute. Let's get things straight. You were one of Planchon's employees, and when you got the chance, you slept with his wife. Were you still living on Rue Lepic?"

"Yes."

"Then one fine day, you moved into the little house on Rue Tholozé, and you more or less shoved Planchon out of bed and took his place."

"Have you seen him?"

"Who?"

"Planchon? You said he was supposed to phone you. So he must have been in touch with you. Did he come and see you? Did he complain about us?"

At such moments in questioning people, Maigret's expression grew vague and his entire personality became irritatingly passive. Now, he did not seem to have heard Prou's question, but gazed absently in the direction of the window. Still drawing on his pipe, he muttered, as if to himself:

"I'm trying to visualize the scene. Planchon comes back

91

home one night and finds a cot set up for him in the dining room. The man's no doubt astonished. Until then, he knew nothing of what was going on behind his back and then, all of a sudden, he discovers that he no longer has the right to sleep in his own bed."

"Do you find that odd?"

Though still outwardly calm, Prou's eyes were hard and bright. Now and again, he could be heard gritting his teeth.

"Do you love her all that much?"

"She's my wife!"

"Legally, she's still Planchon's. Why hasn't your mistress gotten a divorce?"

"Because it takes two to get a divorce, and he keeps stubbornly refusing."

"Does he love her, too?"

"I have no idea. It's nothing to do with me. Go ask him yourself. If you've seen him, you know as well as I do he isn't a real man. He's a nothing. He's a . . ."

He was getting worked up.

"He's Isabelle's father."

"Do you think Isabelle doesn't prefer having me in the house to a fellow who gets drunk every evening, and who sometimes sits and cries on her bed?"

"He didn't drink before you went to work for him."

"Is that what he told you? And you believed him? In that case, there's no point in talking; we're wasting our time. Give me back my paper, ask me the questions you still have to ask, and get it over with. I'm not worried if you've cast me as the villain."

"There's only one thing I don't understand."

"Only one?" he asked ironically.

Slowly and with no expression, Maigret said, as if he hadn't heard:

"It's now a little more than two weeks since Planchon

handed over to you his share in the business. Your mistress and you thereby became the owners. I suppose Planchon never intended to stay and work under your orders?"

"The proof is that he left."

"But he stayed two weeks."

"That surprises you because you seem to believe that people have to act one way or another, according to your own way of thinking. It so happens, this man didn't act your way. Otherwise, he wouldn't have slept for two years on a cot while his wife was sleeping with me in the next room. Don't you understand that?"

"So, after he signed that paper, he knew he'd have to go away?"

"It was agreed between us."

"You had a right to throw him out?"

"I don't know. I'm not a lawyer. The fact remains that we were patient enough to wait two weeks."

As he was listening, Maigret could see the little man with the harelip making his confession in the living room on Boulevard Richard-Lenoir, while behind the glass door the table was ready for supper. Of course, Planchon had been drinking, to give himself courage, he'd said, and Maigret, to help him out, had poured a glass of calvados for him. What he had said, though, rang true.

Yet . . . hadn't Maigret felt slightly uneasy that Saturday night? Hadn't he doubted Planchon and looked at him two or three times, his eyes hardening?

The man's long story contained traces of real passion.

Yet Renée, that morning, though calmer, had been no less passionate.

And Prou was trying to control himself by gritting his teeth.

"Why do you think he came to this sudden decision on Monday evening?"

The man shrugged indifferently.

"Did he have the thirty thousand francs on him?"

"I didn't ask him."

"When you gave them to him, two weeks before, what did he do with them?"

"He went upstairs. I suppose he hid them somewhere."

"Didn't he take them to the bank?"

"Not that day, because it was in the evening, after supper."

"In the office?"

"No. In the living room. We waited until the girl had gone to bed."

"Had you already discussed it together? Was everything agreed between you, including the amount? I suppose you kept the money in the office?"

"No. In the bedroom."

"Afraid he might go off with too much?"

"Because the bedroom is our place."

"You're twenty-nine. You haven't really had time to save much after your military service. How were you able to get so much money in so short a time?"

"I only had part of it. Exactly a third."

"Where did you get the rest?"

He didn't seem at all disconcerted. On the contrary! It was as if he had been waiting for the chief inspector to get to this point. He answered with ill-concealed satisfaction:

"My father lent me ten thousand francs. He's worked long enough to save a mint. And my sister's husband lent me the other ten thousand. His name's Mourier, François Mourier, and he has a butcher shop on Boulevard de Charonne."

"When did you arrange for these loans?"

"On Christmas Eve. We hoped to settle with Planchon the next day."

"Settle with?"

"Give him the money and see him out of the house! You know quite well what I meant."

"I suppose you'd signed receipts?"

"I like things done properly, even in the family."

Maigret passed him a pad and pencil.

"Will you write down the exact addresses of your father and brother-in-law?"

"You really trust me, don't you?"

However, he wrote down the two addresses. His writing was deliberate and neat. Just as the chief inspector took back the pad, the telephone rang.

"Pirouet. I've finished. Do you want to come and see, or would you rather I came down?"

"I'll be up."

Then he said to Prou:

"Will you excuse me a moment?"

He went through to the duty room, left the door open, and told Lapointe:

"Go in and keep an eye on him."

In a short time, he was up under the roof, shaking Moers's hand, and brushing past the dummy used for reconstructions, and on into the laboratory.

Monsieur Pirouet, his face shiny with sweat, was standing in front of two dripping photographic enlargements held up by clothes pins.

"Well?"

"There's something I must ask you, Chief. Does the fellow who signed these papers drink a lot?"

"Why?"

"Because that would explain the difference in the writing. Look first at the signature on the pay slips. The writing isn't very steady. I'd say it belonged to an unstable man who, even so, knows what he's doing. Do you know him?"

"Yes. I had him with me for almost a whole evening."

"Do you want me to give my impression of him?"

Maigret nodded, and he went on:

"He's a man who's had only a primary education, but who's always tried hard. He's almost congenitally shy, yet he has flashes of pride. He tries to appear calm and self-controlled, but in fact he's very emotional. . . ."

"Not bad!"

"There's something wrong with his health. He's ill, or thinks he is."

"How about the signature on the business transfer?"

"That's why I asked you if he drank. The writing's somewhat different. It's maybe the same hand, but in that case whoever signed it was either drunk or under great stress. See for yourself. Compare them. The strokes here are regular, if a bit shaky, as they would be with a man who wasn't actually drunk when he was writing. On the transfer, however, all the letters are jerky."

"Do you think it could be the same man?"

"In the circumstances I've just mentioned, yes. If not, it's a forgery. You often find the same unsteadiness and the same signs of stress in forgeries."

"Thank you. Now, has this writing anything in common with those?"

He showed him the two addresses Roger Prou had written down a few moments before.

Monsieur Pirouet had only to glance at it.

"No connection. I'll explain."

"Not right now. Thank you, Monsieur Pirouet."

Maigret took all the original documents and went back to his office. He found Prou still sitting on his chair, and Lapointe standing in front of the window.

"You can go now," he said to the inspector.

"Well?" Renée's lover asked.

"Nothing. I'll give you back the transfer. I take it that it was typed by Madame Planchon?"

"She told you, didn't she? There's no mystery about it."

"Was her husband drunk when he signed it?"

"He knew what he was doing. We didn't take advantage of him. . . . That doesn't mean he hadn't drunk several brandies. He always had by that time."

"Does your father have a phone? Do you know his number?"

Still looking disdainful, Prou gave him the number. The chief inspector proceeded to dial it.

"His name's Gustave Prou. Don't be afraid to speak up, because he's a little deaf."

"Monsieur Gustave Prou? I'm sorry to trouble you. I'm here with your son. He tells me that, in the month of December, you lent him the sum of ten thousand francs. Yes, I'm with him. . . . What? You want a word with him?"

The old man was suspicious, too. Maigret handed the receiver to Prou.

"It's me, Papa. Do you recognize my voice? Good! You can answer the questions. . . . No, it's just a formality. I'll explain later. See you soon. . . . Yes, everything's all right. Yes, he's gone. Not now. I'll drop by on Sunday."

He handed the receiver back.

"Can you answer my questions now? . . . Did you lend him ten thousand francs? In bills? . . . You drew them from the bank the previous day? From the savings bank? . . . Yes, I can hear you. Did your son sign a receipt? . . . Thank you. Someone will be calling on you. Just to check. All you have to do is show the receipt. . . . Just a moment. What day was it? Christmas Eve?"

Prou's eyes conveyed more irony and contempt than ever.

"I suppose you're going to call my brother-in-law, too?"

"There's no hurry. I don't doubt he'll confirm what you say."

"Can I go?"

"Unless you want to make a statement."

"What statement?"

"I don't know. You might have some idea where Planchon went when he left Rue Tholozé. He's not particularly strong. What's more, he was drunk. He couldn't have gone far, weighted down with two large suitcases."

"That's up to you, isn't it? Or am I expected to find him, too?"

"I'm not asking you to do that. Simply, if you get an idea, to let me know, in order to save time."

"Why didn't you ask Planchon himself when you saw him or when he phoned? He's in a better position to answer than I am."

"Oddly enough, he had no intention of leaving Rue Tholozé."

"Did he say so?"

It was Prou's turn to fish.

"He told me a lot of things."

"Did he come here?"

In spite of his composure, he was looking slightly uncomfortable. Maigret was careful not to answer and to look as blank as possible, as if he had ceased to attach any importance to the conversation.

"There's one thing that puzzles me," he murmured, however.

"What?"

"I don't know if he still loved his wife or if he had begun to loathe her."

"I suppose it changed from time to time."

"How do you mean?"

"According to how drunk he was. He was a different person at different times. Sometimes, we'd stay awake listening to him muttering in the next room and wonder if he was planning to spring some horrible trick on us."

"What sort of trick?"

"Do you want me to spell it out for you? I'll tell you, I always arranged to be on the same job, to keep an eye on him. If, during the day, he mentioned he was going back to Rue Tholozé, I went with him. I was afraid for Renée."

"Do you think he'd be capable of killing her?"

"He went so far as to threaten her."

"With death?"

"Not in so many words, maybe. When he'd been drinking, he used to talk to himself. I couldn't repeat his exact words. They were always a little muddled.

" *'I'm just a coward. All right! Everyone laughs at me. But someday, they'll see that . . .'*

"Get the idea? His eyes would glint with malice. He was like a man who knew what he was doing. Sometimes, he'd suddenly burst out laughing.

" *'Poor Planchon! A poor little insignificant man, with a repellent face. Yet maybe the little man isn't such a coward as all that . . .'* "

Maigret was listening carefully, and felt a slight constriction in his chest because it did not sound made up. The Planchon he had seen on Boulevard Richard-Lenoir and the man Prou was now taking cruel delight in imitating were one and the same person, with barely any exaggeration.

"Do you think he really meant to kill his wife?"

"I'm sure that he thought about it, and at a certain stage of drunkenness, he kept playing with it."

"What about you?"

"Me, too, maybe."

"And his daughter?"

"He probably wouldn't have touched Isabelle. And yet . . . if he could have blown the house up with a bomb . . ."

Maigret got up with a sigh and walked slowly over to the window.

"Hasn't the same idea occurred to you?"

"To kill Renée?"

"Not her. Him!"

"It would certainly be the quickest way of getting rid of him. But, believe me, if I'd intended to, I wouldn't have waited two years. Can you imagine what these two years have been like, with that man constantly around?"

"What about him?"

"He should have realized and gone away. When a woman stops loving you, when she loves someone else, and when she tells you so to your face, you should know what to do."

He got up, too. He was a little less calm. His voice was angrier.

"But that didn't stop him from poisoning our lives, or you from going to question Renée at home, or sending for my employees, or trying to make me say various things for more than an hour. Do you have any more questions to ask? Am I still a free man? Can I go?"

"You can."

"Good-bye, then."

He slammed the door behind him.

7

That evening, Maigret was able to watch television in his warm living room, wearing his bedroom slippers, and with his wife knitting beside him, but he would have liked to be in Janvier's or Lapointe's place. They were in the Montmartre he knew so well, in streets familiar to him, each going his own way, from bistro to bistro, from a yellowish light to a whiter one, from an old-fashioned interior to a more modern one, from the odor of beer to that of calvados.

He had, of course, felt pleased when he'd been promoted and finally become divisional chief inspector of the Criminal Police. But he felt nostalgic about certain beats on which you shivered during winter nights, and about some of the concierges' rooms, with their different smells, which you visited for days on end, forever asking the same, apparently futile, questions.

Up at the top, they reproached him for being too ready to leave his office and go off on his own like a retriever. How could he explain, especially to the examining magistrates, that he had to see things, sniff around, get the feel of a place?

Ironically, tonight the television was showing a tragedy by Corneille. On the little screen, costumed kings and warriors declaimed noble lines, reminding one of schooldays, and it was odd to be interrupted every half hour by the ring of the telephone and to hear Janvier's voice—he was the first to call—this time saying, much less emphatically:

"I think I'm on the track, Chief. I'm calling you from a place on Rue Germain-Pilon, two hundred yards from Place des Abbesses. It's called Au Bon Coin. The owner's already gone to bed. His wife's serving at the bar, and keeps going and sitting by the stove. All I did was mention a man with a harelip and she remembered.

" 'Has something happened to him?' she asked.

"He often used to come and have a couple of drinks here about eight o'clock at night. Apparently, the cat was fond of him and used to rub against his legs. He'd lean down and stroke it.

"It's a small, badly lighted bistro with dark walls. I don't know why it stays open at night, because there's no one here except an oldish man drinking a toddy over by the window."

"Has she seen Planchon since Monday?"

"No. She's pretty sure Monday was the last time he came in. She mentioned to her husband yesterday that they hadn't seen the customer with the harelip and she wondered if he was sick."

"Did he ever confide in her?"

"He hardly ever spoke. She felt sorry for him, thought he looked unhappy, and tried to cheer him up."

"Keep on looking."

Janvier plunged into the cold dark again and, a little farther on, went into another café, and then another. Lapointe was doing the same thing.

Maigret returned to Corneille's characters on the screen. From her armchair, his wife looked at him questioningly.

At half past nine, it was Lapointe's turn to call. He was telephoning from Rue Lepic, from a larger, brighter place, where the regulars were playing cards and where he'd picked up Planchon's scent.

"Still on the brandy, Chief! They knew who he was here, and that he lived on Rue Tholozé, because they'd seen him pass by in the daytime, driving a large van with his name on it in big letters. They felt sorry for him. When he arrived, he was always already half-drunk. He never spoke to anyone. One of the belote players remembered that the last time he came in was on Monday. He ate two hard-boiled eggs from the wire holder on the counter."

Janvier must have chosen the wrong route, because, soon after, he telephoned that he'd had no luck in five bistros. They had never heard of the man with the harelip.

Singers, male and female, had taken over from Corneille's heroes on the screen when, about eleven o'clock, Lapointe called for the second time. He seemed excited.

"I've got news, Chief. But I wonder if we might not do better to meet at the Quai des Orfèvres. I'm watching a woman through the door, and I'm afraid she'll slip away."

"No. Tell me now."

"I'm in a brasserie on Plaee Blanche. The terrace is glassed in and heated by two braziers. Are you still there?"

"I'm listening."

"The first waiter I spoke to knows Planchon well by sight. Apparently, he always used to come here fairly late in the evening, and, more often than not, wasn't too steady on his legs. He used to sit on the terrace and order a beer."

"Presumably to chase down all the brandies he'd drunk elsewhere."

"I don't know if you know this place. There are two or

three women on the terrace most of the time, watching the passersby. They work mainly at the cinema exit next door.

"The waiter pointed one of them out to me.

" 'Here! You have a word with Sylvie. That's her name. She'll tell you more than I can. I've seen them go off together a few times.'

"She guessed right away I was from the police, and at first she didn't want to say anything.

" 'What has he done?' she asked. 'Why are you looking for him? Why do you think I should know him?'

"Little by little, she began to talk, and I think what she said will interest you. I even think it would be best to get a written statement from her while she's in a good mood. What shall I do?"

"Take her to the P.J. I'll be there about the same time as you."

Madame Maigret resignedly went to get him his shoes.

"Do you want me to call a taxi?"

"Yes, please."

He put on his overcoat and didn't forget his scarf. He had just drunk a toddy, because he felt now that he was in for a good bout of flu.

At the Quai des Orfèvres, he saluted the lone policeman on duty at the street door, climbed the broad gray staircase, and walked along the empty corridor. After he switched on the light in his office, he pushed open the door of the duty room.

Lapointe was there, still wearing his hat, and a woman got up from the chair on which she'd been sitting.

At that moment, all over Paris, hundreds of women who might have been her sisters were walking the streets, in the shadows, not far from furnished hotels with front doors discreetly ajar.

She was wearing exaggeratedly high stiletto heels, and her

legs were thin. The entire lower half of her body was long and slender. She broadened only at the hips, and the disparity was more striking because she was wearing a short coat, made of some long-haired fur that looked like goat's hair.

Her face was like a doll's, bright pink, with coal-black eyelashes.

"Mademoiselle was good enough to accompany me," said Lapointe pleasantly.

She replied ironically but unmaliciously:

"As if you wouldn't have carted me off anyway!"

She seemed impressed by the chief inspector and looked him up and down.

He took off his coat and motioned to her to sit. Lapointe settled himself in front of a typewriter, ready to take down her statement.

"What's your name?"

"Antoinette Lesourd. I'm usually called Sylvie. Antoinette sounds old-fashioned. It's my grandmother's name, and . . ."

"Do you know Planchon?"

"I didn't know his name till tonight. He used to come to the brasserie most every evening, and he was always well-oiled. At first, I thought he was a widower drowning his sorrows. He seemed so unhappy."

"Did he speak to you first?"

"No. I did. The first time, I was quite sure he was going to run away. But I said: 'I've got troubles, too. I know what it's like. I was married to a bum who went off one fine day, with my daughter.'

"It was when I mentioned my daughter that he suddenly softened up."

Turning to Lapointe, she said:

"You're not putting all that down!"

"Only the essentials," Maigret put in. "When did you start to talk to him?"

"Let's see. In the summer I worked in Cannes, because the American fleet was in. I came back here in September. So I must have met him about the beginning of October."

"Did he follow you the first evening?"

"No. He bought me a drink. Then he told me he had to get home, that he got up early because of his work, and that it was late. He didn't follow me until two or three days later."

"Back to your place?"

"I never have anyone at my place. The concierge wouldn't allow it. It's a respectable house. In fact, there's a judge living on the second floor. I usually go to a hotel on Rue Lepic. Do you know it? . . . Whatever you do, don't make it awkward for them. With all the new regulations, you never quite know where you are."

"Did Planchon often go with you?"

"Not often. Maybe a dozen times in all. And even then he didn't always do anything."

"Did he talk?"

"He once said: 'You see! They're right. I'm not even a man.' "

"Didn't he mention any details about his life?"

"I spotted his wedding ring, of course. One evening I asked him: 'Is it your wife who's giving you hell?'

"He said that his wife hadn't deserved to meet a man like him."

"When did you see him last?"

Maigret could tell from the way Lapointe, still at the typewriter, winked that he had got to the interesting part.

"Monday evening."

"How can you be sure it was Monday?"

"Because on Monday I got pinched and spent twenty-four hours in the lockup. You can ask your boys. My name must be down on the list. They had a Black Maria full."

"What time on Monday did he get to the brasserie?"

"It was almost ten. I'd just come out, because there's no point in starting early in Montmartre."

"What state was he in?"

"He could hardly walk. I saw right away that he'd had more to drink than usual. He came and sat next to me on the terrace, near the brazier. He couldn't even raise his arm to call the waiter. He just stammered: 'A brandy. And a brandy for madame.'

"We almost fought. I didn't want him to drink more alcohol, in the state he was, but he kept on.

" 'I'm ill,' he kept saying. 'Nothing like a large brandy to take care of it.' "

"Did he say anything else that struck you?"

Another wink from Lapointe.

"Yes. A few words I didn't understand. He said, two or three times: 'He won't believe me, either.' "

"Didn't he explain?"

"He mumbled: 'Don't worry. I know what I'm doing. And you'll understand, too, someday.' "

Maigret remembered the tone in which Planchon, the same Monday, a few hours before this scene, had spoken to him over the telephone, while he was still on Place des Abbesses:

"Thank you."

He hadn't sensed merely the bitterness and disillusion, but some kind of threat, too.

"Did you go to the hotel together?"

"He wanted to. But when we got outside, he fell flat on the sidewalk. I helped him get up. He was humiliated.

" 'I'll show them I'm a man,' he muttered.

"I had to hold him up. I knew the hotel manager wouldn't let him in the way he was, and I didn't want him to be sick in the room, either.

" 'Where do you live?' I asked him.

" 'Up there.'

" 'Where's up there?'

" 'Rue Tho . . . Rue Tho . . .'

"He could hardly get his words out.

" 'Rue Tholozé?'

" 'Yes. Straight ahead . . . Straight ahead . . .'

"It isn't always fun, I can tell you. I was afraid a *flic* might spot us and think I was trying to rob him. They'd obviously have made out that I'd forced him to drink. I don't want to say bad things about the police, but you must admit they sometimes . . ."

"Go on. Did you call a taxi?"

"Are you joking? I was broke. I helped him walk. It took us almost half an hour to get to the end of Rue Tholozé, because he kept stopping, his legs kept buckling, and he kept saying, at every bistro, that a large brandy would fix him up. Finally he stopped in front of an iron gate, and fell down again. The gate wasn't shut. There was a van in the yard, with a name on it I couldn't make out in the dark. I didn't leave him till we reached the door."

"Were the lights on inside?"

"There was some light showing through the blinds on the ground floor. I propped him up against the wall, hoping he'd stay on his feet for a while, rang the bell, and left as fast as I could."

All the while she'd been talking, the typewriter kept tapping away.

"Has something happened to him?"

"He's disappeared."

"I hope you're not going to think it was me?"

"Don't worry."

"Do you think they'll send me up in front of the judge?"

"I hope not. But even if they did, you'd have nothing to worry about."

Lapointe removed the sheet of paper from the typewriter and handed it to the woman.

"Do I have to read it?"

"And sign it."

"I won't have any trouble?"

She eventually signed her name, in large, clumsy letters.

"What shall I do now?"

"You're free to go."

"Do you think I can still get a bus?"

Maigret took some money from his pocket.

"Here. For a taxi."

She had hardly left when the phone rang. It was Janvier, who had called the apartment on Boulevard Richard-Lenoir. Madame Maigret had told him that her husband was at the PJ.

"Nothing, Chief. I've done Boulevard Rochechouart as far as Place d'Anvers. I've been up at least a dozen side streets."

"You can go to bed now."

"Has Lapointe found something?"

"Yes. We'll tell you tomorrow."

When Maigret got home, there was one thing he was afraid of: waking up next morning with a temperature. He still had an unpleasant tickling sensation in his nose and he felt as if his eyelids were burning. What was worse, his pipe did not taste the same.

His wife made him another toddy, and he perspired all night.

At nine o'clock in the morning, he was sitting, somewhat light-headed, in the deputy prosecutor's anteroom, where he waited a good twenty minutes.

He must have looked depressed, because Méchin asked him:

"Did the fellow you called in make trouble?"

"No. But there are new developments."

"Have you found your decorator? What was his name again?"

"Planchon. No, we haven't found him. We've been able to reconstruct how he spent his time on Monday evening. When he got back home, shortly before eleven o'clock at night, he was so drunk he couldn't stand up; he fell down several times between Place Blanche, where he had his last drink, and Rue Tholozé."

"Was he alone?"

"A prostitute, with whom he'd gone to a hotel several times, got him home."

"Do you believe her?"

"I'm sure she's telling the truth. She rang the bell of the house before she went away, leaving Planchon more or less propped against the wall. It's impossible that, a few minutes later, he went upstairs, filled two suitcases with his things, carried them downstairs, and then walked to the street."

"He might have taken something to sober himself up. Such things exist."

"His wife and Prou would have mentioned it."

"Prou's the lover, isn't he? The one you called in? What does he say?"

Slowly and patiently, still dizzy, Maigret told the story of the thirty thousand francs and the receipts, including the one signed by Planchon.

"Monsieur Pirouet, our handwriting expert, isn't certain. In his opinion, it could have been signed by Planchon when drunk, but the result would have been similar if the signature had been supplied by someone else."

"What about the other receipts?"

"On December 24, Prou borrowed twenty thousand francs, ten from his father and ten from his brother-in-law. One of my men photographed the receipts. The one held by the brother-in-law states that the sum is to be repaid in five years, and that Prou is to pay interest at six percent. The father's, on the other hand, provided for repayment in two years and doesn't mention any interest."

"Do you think they're goodwill receipts?"

"No. My men checked. On December 23, the day before the payment, Prou's father drew ten thousand francs in bills from his savings bank account, in which he has just over twenty thousand. The brother-in-law, Mourier, drew the same amount, on the same day, from his post office account."

"But I thought you mentioned thirty thousand francs?"

"The third ten thousand was drawn by Roger Prou from his own account, with Crédit Lyonnais. So, on that date, there were thirty thousand francs, legal tender, in the house on Rue Tholozé."

"On what date was the transfer document signed?"

"December 29. It all took place as if Prou and his mistress had planned everything well before Christmas, and were waiting for the right opportunity to get the husband to sign the document."

"In that case, I don't see . . ."

As if to make things more difficult, Maigret added:

"Monsieur Pirouet has analyzed the ink of the signature. He can't date it precisely, but he's sure it's more than two weeks old."

"What do you intend to do? Drop the case?"

"I've come to ask you for a search warrant."

"After what you've just told me?"

Maigret nodded, not too proud of himself.

"What do you expect to find in the house? Planchon's corpse?"

"It's hardly likely."

"The money?"

"I don't know."

"Must you really?"

"Planchon was incapable of walking at eleven o'clock on Monday."

"Wait here a moment. I can't take the responsibility. I'll have a word or two with the public prosecutor."

Maigret waited alone for about ten minutes.

"He doesn't like it much, either, especially right now, when the police aren't having a very good press. . . ."

Anyway, the answer was yes, and, a moment or two later, the chief inspector went off with a signed warrant. It was ten minutes to ten. He whipped open the door of the duty room, couldn't see Lapointe, but spotted Janvier.

"Get a car from the yard. I'll be right down."

Then he called the Crime Squad and gave instructions to Moers.

"Get them there as quickly as you can. And pick the best."

He went downstairs and got into the little black car beside Janvier.

"Rue Tholozé."

"Did you get the warrant?"

"I dragged it out of them. . . . I'd rather not think what's in store for me if there's nothing there, and if the wife or her lover kick up the dust."

He was plunged so deeply in thought that he hardly noticed that the sun had come out, for the first time in several days. Janvier went on talking as they dodged in and out around buses and taxis.

"People like him don't work on Saturdays, as a rule. I think it's forbidden by the unions, unless they get double pay. There's a chance we may find Prou at home."

He was not there. It was Renée who came and opened the door, after glancing at them through the window. She was more suspicious and disagreeable than ever.

"You again!" she exclaimed.

"Isn't Prou here?"

"He's gone to finish an urgent job. What do you want this time?"

Maigret took the warrant from his pocket and gave it to her to read.

"You're going to search the house? Well, really, that's the limit!"

A Crime Squad van, full of men and equipment, drove into the yard.

"And who are these people?"

"My colleagues. I'm sorry, but it'll take us some time."

"Will you make a mess?"

"I'm afraid so."

"Are you sure you have the right?"

"The warrant's signed by the deputy public prosecutor." She shrugged.

"That's a great help. I don't even know what that is."

However, she let them in, giving them all black looks.

"I hope it will be over by the time my daughter gets back from school."

"That depends."

"On what?"

"On what we find."

"If you'd only tell me what you're looking for . . ."

"Your husband definitely left with two suitcases on Monday evening, didn't he?"

"I told you that before."

"I suppose he took with him the thirty thousand francs Prou paid him on December 29?"

"I have no idea. We gave him the money, but it wasn't our business what he did with it."

"He didn't put it in his bank account."

"Did you check up?"

"Yes. You said he had no friends. So it's unlikely that he trusted that amount to any person."

"What are you hinting at?"

"He couldn't have been walking around with that amount on him ever since December 29. Thirty thousand francs is a large bundle."

"So?"

"Nothing."

"Is that what you're looking for?"

"I don't know."

The experts were already at work, beginning with the kitchen. It was a job they were used to, and they went about it methodically, leaving no stone unturned, searching cans containing flour, sugar, and coffee as well as the garbage can.

It all went so smoothly that it looked like a kind of ballet, and the woman watched them with surprise, almost bewildered.

"Who's going to clear it all up?"

Maigret didn't answer.

"Can I make a phone call?" she asked.

She called an apartment on Rue Lamarck, belonging to a Madame Fajon, and asked to speak to the housepainter who was working there.

"Is that you? They've come back. The chief inspector, yes, and a crowd of men, who are turning the house upside down. Some of them are even taking photographs. . . . No. Apparently they've got a warrant. They showed me a paper supposed to have been signed by a deputy something. . . . Yes. I'd rather you came back."

She gave Maigret an ugly look, which contained a hint of defiance.

One of the men was scratching at some stains on the floor of the dining room and collecting the dust he got in a little bag.

"What's he doing? Doesn't he think my floor's clean enough?"

Another man was tapping the walls with an upholsterer's hammer. Photographs and reproductions of paintings were taken down one after another, and then replaced, somewhat crookedly.

Two men had gone up to the second floor, where they could be heard walking around.

"Are they going to do the same in my daughter's room?"

"I'm afraid so."

"What shall I tell Isabelle when she gets back?"

It was the first time that Maigret had joked:

"That we've been playing treasure hunt. . . . Haven't you got a television?"

"No. We would have bought one next month."

"Why 'would have'?"

"Would have, will, what's the difference? If you think I'm in any state to choose my words . . ."

She suddenly recognized Janvier.

"When I think that he came and measured all the rooms in the house on some excuse . . ."

They heard the van enter the yard, its door slam, and rapid footsteps. Renée must have recognized them, because she immediately moved to the door.

"Look!" she said to Roger Prou. "They're going through everything, including my pans and linen. They're upstairs in the girl's room, too."

Prou's lips quivered with fury as he looked the chief inspector up and down.

"Do you have the right to do this?" he asked, his voice unsteady.

Maigret handed him the warrant.

"What if I phoned a lawyer?"

"It's your right. But all he could do is be present at the search."

About noon, there was a rattle at the mail slot, and,

through the window, Maigret saw that Isabelle had arrived home. Her mother rushed off and, with the girl, shut herself in the kitchen, where the Crime Squad had finished its work.

No doubt some interesting things would have come to light if he had questioned the little girl, but, except in cases of absolute necessity, Maigret loathed interrogating children.

The office had been searched without result. A few of the men moved toward the shed in the yard, and one of them climbed into the van.

It was a fine-tooth-comb search by men with much experience.

"Will you come up here, Chief?"

Prou, who had heard this, followed Maigret up the stairs.

A child's bedroom, with a teddy bear on the bed, looked as if it were moving day. The wardrobe and mirror had been shoved into a corner, along with the rest of the furniture. The men had pulled up the reddish linoleum that covered the floor.

One of the floorboards had been pried up.

"Look here."

But Maigret first looked at Prou's face. He was standing in the doorway. His face had grown so hard that the chief inspector yelled:

"Watch out, down there."

But Prou did not make a run for it, as might have been expected. Nor did he move into the room, or even bother to bend over the hole in the floor, at the bottom of which was a newspaper-wrapped package.

Nothing was touched until the photographer came and fingerprints on the grayish boards were taken.

At last Maigret was able to bend down, pick up the package, and open it. There were bundles of hundred-franc bills, three of them, and one of the bundles was crisp and new.

"Have you anything to say, Prou?"

"I know nothing about it."

"Wasn't it you who put the money in this hiding place?"

"Why should I have?"

"Do you maintain that on Monday evening your former employer left here with two suitcases containing his things, yet didn't take the thirty thousand francs?"

"I have nothing to say."

"Wasn't it you who raised the linoleum, pried up a floorboard, and hid the money?"

"I know nothing more than what I told you yesterday."

"Was it your mistress?"

He gave a rather hesitant glance.

"What she may or may not have done is no concern of mine."

8

"What she may or may not have done is no concern of mine."

These words, the tone in which they were said, and the glance that acccompanied them lingered in Maigret's mind during the months that followed.

That Saturday, there were lights at the Quai des Orfèvres until the small hours of the morning. The chief inspector, moving carefully, had advised both the lovers to designate a lawyer. Since they didn't know any, they had been given a list of members of the bar, and they had chosen at random.

In this way, regulations had been strictly observed. One of the lawyers, Renée's, was young and fair-haired, and she immediately began, in spite of herself, to turn her charm on him. Prou's, by contrast, was middle-aged, with a clumsily knotted tie, grubby shirt, and dirty fingernails, who could be seen touting for clients all day long in the corridors of the Palais de Justice.

Ten, twenty, a hundred times, Maigret repeated the same

questions, sometimes to Renée Planchon alone, sometimes to Prou, sometimes to both together.

At first, each seemed to consult the other's face. Then, as the questioning went on, and when they'd been separated for some while before being brought together again, their looks grew more suspicious.

When he had seen them the first time, Maigret had been reminded, not without some admiration, of a couple of wild animals.

The couple no longer existed. They remained two wild animals, though, and it began to look as if it wouldn't be long before they tore each other to pieces.

"Who struck your husband?"

"I have no idea. I don't know that he *was* struck. I went to my bedroom as soon as he left."

"You told me . . ."

"I know nothing more than what I've said. You confuse me with all your questions."

"Did you know that the thirty thousand francs were in your daughter's bedroom?"

"No."

"Didn't you hear your lover move the furniture, raise the linoleum, and pry up a floorboard?"

"I'm not at home all the time. I keep telling you I don't know anything. You can question me as long as you like, but I have nothing else to say."

"And you didn't hear the van leave the yard on the night of Monday to Tuesday?"

"No."

"Yet the neighbors heard it."

"Good for them."

It was not true. Maigret had resorted to a somewhat crude trick. The concierge in the next building had not heard anything. Of course, her room was on the side away from the yard. They had questioned the neighbors without any success.

Meanwhile, Prou repeated obstinately what he had told the chief inspector during his first interrogation at the Quai des Orfèvres.

"I was asleep when he came. Renée got up and went into the living room. I heard them talk for quite a while. Someone went upstairs."

"Weren't you listening behind the door?"

"I've told you the truth."

"Did you hear everything that was going on?"

"Not very well."

"Could your mistress have knocked Planchon down without your knowing it?"

"I went back to bed and right to sleep."

"Before your ex-boss left?"

"I don't know."

"Didn't you hear the outside door close?"

"I didn't hear a thing."

The lawyers nodded; each one adopted his client's position.

At five in the morning, Prou and his mistress were taken away, separately, to the cells under the Palais de Justice. Maigret went to bed, but for only an hour. After drinking five or six cups of black coffee, he went once again to the Public Prosecutor's Office, a place too solemn for his taste. This time, although it was a Sunday, he was permitted an interview with the public prosecutor himself. They remained closeted nearly two hours.

"The body still hasn't been discovered?"

"No."

"No bloodstains in the house or the van?"

"None yet found."

With no corpse, it was impossible to charge the couple with murder. There remained the money, which, as the transfer document proved, belonged to Planchon. There was no reason why it should be hidden under Isabelle's floorboards.

She had been taken to a children's home.

Maigret was allowed another three hours of questioning, on Monday morning, once again in front of the lawyers, after which an examining magistrate took over the case. This was the new method, to which he was now resigned.

Was the examining magistrate any happier about the case than he was? He had no idea; the man did not bother to keep him up to date.

But only a week later, a body was pulled from the Seine, at the Suresnes dam. About a dozen people—in particular, the owners of the Montmartre bistros Planchon had visited in the evening, and the girl called Sylvie—identified him.

Prou and Renée, taken separately to see the decomposed body, kept their mouths closed.

According to the police doctor, Planchon had been killed by several blows on the head with a heavy instrument probably wrapped in a cloth.

He had then been tied up in a sack. Later, there was a battle between experts about the sack and the cord around it. They had found similar sacks in the shed in the yard, as well as some cord used to tie up ladders, which seemed to be made of the same stuff.

Maigret knew nothing about all this for several months. Spring had been around long enough for the chestnut trees to burst into flower. Men were going around without coats. A young Englishman was identified as the jewel thief in the big hotels, and Interpol was on his track in Australia; a few of the missing stones, removed from their settings, were recovered in Italy.

The Planchon affair reached the courts only a few days before the judicial holiday, and Maigret found himself closeted in the witnesses' room with a certain number of people he knew and others he did not.

When it was his turn to go into the witness box, he realized, from his first glance at the accused, that Renée Planchon and Roger Prou's passion had been transformed into hatred.

They defended themselves to save their own skins, and were ready to let suspicion rest on the other. They glared viciously at each other.

"Do you swear to tell the truth, the whole truth, and nothing but the truth?"

With his hand, Maigret repeated a gesture he had made often in these surroundings.

"I do!"

"Tell the jury what you know about the case."

The accused were once again staring at him resentfully. Wasn't it he who had started the investigation, and didn't they owe their arrest to him?

It was obvious that the act had been premeditated and had been worked out some time before. Prou had been clever enough to borrow the twenty thousand francs on December 24, from his father and his brother-in-law.

Wouldn't it be natural to buy the business he was working for from a drunkard who was no longer able to cope?

The receipts were genuine. The money had been paid.

But Planchon had never known anything about it. He never had any idea what was being hatched in his own house. Even though he had felt that they wanted to get rid of him, he had never dreamed that the process had already begun, or that on December 29, or around that time, his wife was typing out a counterfeit transfer document, at the bottom of which someone would forge his signature.

Who? Renée or her lover?

The experts were to have interminable arguments and some bittersweet exchanges about that, too.

"On a Saturday evening . . ." Maigret began.

"Speak up."

"On a Saturday evening, when I returned home, about seven, I found a man waiting for me."

"Did you know him?"

"I didn't, but I guessed who he was right away because of his harelip. For almost two months, a man answering to his description had been coming to see me at the Quai des Orfèvres on Saturday afternoons, but he always disappeared before I had a chance to see him."

"Do you solemnly swear that it was Léonard Planchon?"

"Yes."

"What did he want?"

As he faced the jury, the chief inspector turned his back on the two accused, so that he could not see their reactions.

They must have been dumbfounded when they realized that he was going to help them out.

In complete silence, followed by such an uproar that the judge had to threaten to clear the court, Maigret said clearly:

"He wanted to tell me that he intended to kill his wife and her lover."

In theory, he would have liked to say he felt sorry for poor old Planchon. But a few moments before, he had sworn to tell the truth, the whole truth, and nothing but the truth.

Once order was restored, he was able to answer the judge's detailed questions, and, his evidence concluded, he did not really have time to hang around the courtroom. He had just been told that a crime had been committed in a luxury apartment on Rue Lauriston.

There were no confessions. Yet the charges were overwhelming enough for the jury to answer the first question in the affirmative.

Ironically, it was Maigret's statement that saved Roger Prou's neck and won him "extenuating circumstances."

"You have heard the chief inspector's statement," his lawyer pleaded. "It was one man or the other. Even though my client killed, it was in legal self-defense."

Antoinette, the girl with the long thin legs and broad hips they called Sylvie, was in court when the foreman of the jury read out the verdict.

Twenty years for Roger Prou and eight for Renée Planchon, who glared at her former lover with such loathing that a shiver passed through the courtroom. . . .

"Did you read this, Chief?"

Janvier showed Maigret a recent newspaper with the verdict on the front page.

The chief inspector glanced at it and merely growled:

"Poor wretch!"

He felt he had betrayed the man with the harelip, whose last words on the telephone had, however, been:

"Thank you!"